YESTERDAY LOVE

YESTERDAY LOVE

Juliet Gray

Chivers Press   •   G.K. Hall & Co.
Bath, Avon, England   Thorndike, Maine USA

This Large Print edition is published by Chivers Press, England and by G.K. Hall & Co., USA.

Published in 1996 in the U.K. by arrangement with the author.

Published in 1996 in the U.S. by arrangement with Laurence Pollinger, Ltd.

U.K. Hardcover ISBN 0–7451–3879–9 (Chivers Large Print)
U.K. Softcover ISBN 0–7451–3890–X (Camden Large Print)
U.S. Softcover ISBN 0–7838–1449–6 (Nightingale Collection Edition)

The text of this Large Print edition is unabridged.
Other aspects of the book may vary from the original edition.

Set in 16 pt. New Times Roman.

Printed in Great Britain on acid-free paper.

British Library Cataloguing in Publication Data available

Library of Congress Cataloging-in-Publication Data

Gray, Juliet.
  Yesterday love / Juliet Gray.
    p.   cm.
  ISBN 0–7838–1449–6 (lg. print : lsc)
  1. Large type books.   I. Title.
[PR6057.R3268Y47   1996]
823'.914—dc20
                                                                    95–30273

YESTERDAY LOVE

CHAPTER ONE

She was very beautiful with something more than the beauty that is the right of every bride—and soon she would be the wife of one of the wealthiest and most successful men in England.

She stared at the reflection in the long mirror of a very slender girl in a delicious creation of frothing white tulle and lace that emphasised the pale blonde beauty of hair and skin—and enormous dark-blue eyes stared back at her, wide and anxious. She had entered into all the plans and preparations of the past weeks as though it was all happening to someone else, eager, excited, almost ecstatic. But now, quite suddenly, she knew that it was herself, Abigail Carr, who was being prepared for the ritual sacrifice of marriage—and something very like panic rose in her breast.

Her cousin Kate was one of the foremost fashion designers of the day and the lovely gown was of her creating. The dress was a jealously guarded secret for this had been talked about as the Wedding of the Year ever since it had first been announced and she was determined that her young cousin should be one of the loveliest brides ever to walk down the aisle ... and equally determined that the bridal gown should be *the* talking-point of the

1

day. Only her most trusted seamstress had helped in the actual making of the gown. Kate had done much of the work herself, and now she was intent on supervising the final fitting.

'I can't!' Abigail said abruptly, a little desperately. 'Kate, I can't! Whatever am I doing!' She began to fumble with the tiny pearl buttons that fastened the long sleeves at her slender wrists, her fingers trembling as another wave of panic swept over her.

'What are you doing, indeed,' Kate returned rather absently, too intent on studying the fall of the hem to notice the desperation in her cousin's voice. She slapped lightly at Abigail's hand. 'Now don't fuss, Abby—those sleeves are just right!' She sat back on her heels, a slight frown in her dark, intelligent eyes, her short silky cap of dark hair almost on end where she habitually thrust her slender fingers through it as an aid to concentration. 'I think ... just half an inch higher, after all,' she decided. 'We don't want you to trip on your way down the aisle and land at Max's feet, do we?'

'I want to take it off,' Abigail said in a low, urgent voice.

'So you shall in just one moment...' Her deft fingers busy with pins, Kate frowned in acute concentration, deaf to the urgency and rising panic in her cousin's words.

'Kate! You aren't listening!' Abigail's voice rose on a little sob of near-hysteria. 'I can't do it! I'm not going through with it! I can't marry Max!'

Her cousin's attention was finally caught. Her hands stilled, she looked up at the pale and troubled face, the apprehensive eyes—and then she smiled reassuringly. 'Last-minute nerves,' she said, understanding. 'It happens to every bride, darling—and the men are just as bad! Max is probably pacing up and down this very minute wondering if he can go through with it after all! Don't worry, Abby. Everything will be fine! You'll be the happiest girl in the world when you marry Max tomorrow morning!'

Abigail clenched her hands so fiercely that the long and beautifully-kept nails dug tiny crescents into her palms. 'I can't help worrying and everything *won't* be fine! Kate, you don't understand! It's all quite dreadful! Kate, I don't love him,' she announced with a little gasp.

It seemed astonishing now that she had ever supposed that she loved Max and wanted to marry him. Suddenly she had discovered that her feeling for him was not in the least like loving and that he was the last man in the world that she wanted for a husband. It had been a pleasant but totally unreal dream all these weeks—but the wedding that was due to take place only the next day was stark reality! Realisation had hit her like a blow to the stomach. She was sick, shocked and very scared...

3

Kate was silent for a moment. Then she rose from her knees and began to help Abigail out of the lovely wedding dress. She said lightly: 'Love him? Well, what has that to say to anything, for heaven's sake? You're marrying *Max Constantine*, sweetie—and I know a dozen women who'd give anything to be standing in your shoes! You don't have to love him, Abby—just be thankful that he wants to marry you!'

Abigail stared. 'Thankful!'

'Max could have married anyone,' Kate said with truth. 'All he had to do was lift a finger.' She carefully smoothed the folds of the lovely gown while Abigail reached for a robe and wrapped it about her slender body. 'He has been London's most eligible bachelor for years!'

'Yes, I know,' Abigail said wearily, no longer impressed. She pushed strands of long, shining hair from her face and sank into a chair, feeling desperately tired. For weeks she had been under a strain, playing a part ... but she had only just realised it, she thought bleakly.

'Not as *I* know,' Kate declared firmly. 'I don't think you really appreciate what a feather in your cap it is to have caught Max Constantine of all men! I've seen many girls casting out lures to him for the past ten years and there's never been the least hint of a serious affair. He just isn't a marrying man—or wasn't

4

until you came along. You must be very special, Abby,' she added with just a hint of betraying envy in her tone.

Abigail shrugged. 'I used to think so,' she said with the candour of a noted beauty who saw no point in denying the obvious. 'But there are some exceptionally lovely women among Max's circle of friends—and I'm sure all of them are more suitable than I am to be Lady Constantine!'

'Possibly,' Kate said briskly. 'But the man happens to want you, Abby.' She laid the dress in folds upon folds of tissue in the big box.

'Yes—and I'm flattered, of course,' Abigail said wryly. 'He's so attractive and very nice and I do like him. It was exciting that he took such notice of me and perhaps I was a little infatuated at first—oh, I don't know! I was over the moon when he proposed and I said yes without really thinking—Max Constantine wanting to marry *me*! Oh, you know, Kate! I've been doing a lot of thinking just lately,' she added ruefully.

There was irony in the twist of Kate's smile. 'It's a pity your mental processes couldn't wait another twenty-four hours,' she said drily. 'So you've been thinking—about the kind of man he is and the life he's led and the women he's had and you wonder if you can make him happy and what demands he'll make on you and if you can possibly be right for each other ... and you've thought yourself into a

5

stupid panic.'

'Yes, I suppose so ... something like that, anyway,' Abigail admitted.

'I know, sweetie. I've been through it all myself,' Kate said with warm understanding.

She seldom mentioned the marriage that had ended in divorce and Abigail was reluctant to probe. She was just a little in awe of her clever and sophisticated cousin. But she could not resist saying, a little shyly: 'You were in love with Silas when you married him, weren't you?'

'Yes—and what a mess of a marriage that turned out to be,' Kate said briskly. 'You're more likely to be happy without love to complicate matters, my child!' She took a Gauloise from its pack and spun a slender gold cigarette lighter to life.

Abigail did not smoke and she disliked the smell of tobacco and she particularly disliked the strong smell of the French cigarettes that her cousin affected—and in her bedroom of all places! But she was much too polite to protest and merely determined to fling wide all the windows as soon as Kate went away.

'I couldn't possibly be happy living with someone I don't love,' she said quietly. 'I should hate it!'

Kate smiled, realising how very young and inexperienced and unsophisticated she was ... and wondering if Max really knew what he was about! She was very fond of Abigail but it was

6

extremely difficult to imagine her as the wife of someone like Max who had always chosen the most elegant and most worldly of women as his companions in the past. But Max had obviously decided that it was time he married if only for an heir to his title and estates—and men like Max did not marry the kind of woman they chose as a mistress, Kate thought cynically. They married innocents like her cousin Abigail, young and presentable and of good family. She had birth and breeding as well as beauty. She had been educated at the right schools and knew all the right people and she would be a valuable asset to him. She would run his home efficiently and preside over his table gracefully and dutifully present him with a couple of attractive and well-behaved children in time—and she would not expect too much of him or interfere with his way of life as might a woman who was not quite so well-bred!

Kate was amused by Abigail's insistence on love. Certainly no one supposed that she was in love with Max and no one wondered at her willingness to marry him. Nor did anyone imagine that he had fallen headlong in love with a sweet innocent so much younger than himself. No doubt he was attracted by her loveliness and perhaps he was intrigued by her innocence but it seemed to Kate and to others that he would very soon become bored with his young bride.

7

She said lightly, confidently: 'My dear Abby, I daresay you'll fall in and out of love a dozen times ... but there's only one Max. I don't blame you for feeling nervous. That's quite natural. But I shall suppose you the world's biggest idiot if you jilt him now ... and I wouldn't want the task of breaking the news to your mother!' she added with feeling. Her gaze rested on the small, troubled face that was lovely enough to have captivated a much less susceptible man than Max Constantine. She went on easily: 'I daresay you're fonder of him than you think just now. I've seen you together too often to believe that you're indifferent to him and he certainly thinks the world of you.'

Abigail teased the knotted fringe of her robe with restless fingers. 'Does he?' she said quietly and with a good deal of doubt in her voice. Kate might confidently suppose that Max cared for her but he had yet to say so, she thought wryly. He said many things in his smooth, lighthearted way for he was an experienced flirt and she knew all about his reputation as a rake. But he had never once said that he loved her—not even when he had asked her to marry him! She was very inclined to believe that it was a marriage of convenience for him!

Kate felt swift impatience with Max who had handled matters very badly if he had not managed to convince her trusting little cousin that he was very much in love. Surely a man

8

with his experience should have realised that such a naive innocent would want to believe it a love match rather than a marriage of mutual advantage! No wonder Abby was ready to cry off on the day before the wedding! No wonder she was filled with doubts and fears and nervous apprehensions for the future!

She looked at Abigail for a moment. Then she said gently: 'What's really wrong, Abby? Is it sex? No need to be shy with me, you know. Has Max frightened you? He's a very passionate man and perhaps he doesn't realise that you're not as experienced as other women he's known.'

The hot colour flooded her face. She rose and went to a window, throwing it wide so that the breeze might cool her hot cheeks and also sweeten the tobacco-scented atmosphere of her bedroom. Kate had it very wrong, she thought wryly. She had not found Max to be an impatient or ardent lover . . . and the lack of fire in his embrace and the lack of urgency in his kiss seemed to imply that he found her much less exciting than all those other women he had known before her.

She was very sure that he did not love her or want her at all. He merely needed a wife and he had looked around for a green girl that he could mould into the kind of wife that would suit him. Of course, it was important that she should not be just any girl but one like herself with the right looks, the right background, the right connections. Swept off her feet by the glamour and the undeniable charm of the man, by the flattery of his attentions, she had played right into his hands, she thought ruefully—and he had not even needed to pretend non-existent feelings, to play the part of lover as well as would-be husband.

'That isn't the problem,' she said stiffly, finding it impossible to explain the mingled relief and resentment at his lack of sexual interest where she was concerned.

'Sexual compatibility can be more important than loving each other,' Kate said quietly. 'Are you and Max compatible in that way, Abby?'

Abigail shrugged. 'I don't know.' Her tone held impatience. 'How would I know? He treats me like a piece of porcelain!'

Surprise flickered in Kate's eyes. 'How he has changed,' she said drily. 'Max of all men!'

Abigail turned swiftly. 'So it seems,' she said tartly. 'Apparently I'm about to marry the worst rake in town—and I wish I understood why everyone is pushing me into it with both hands!'

'We have your interests at heart, my child,' Kate said lightly. 'Reformed rakes make the best husbands.'

'I wish I could believe that marriage will have a reforming influence on him!' Abigail retorted.

'Max will make an excellent husband—as

10

long as you don't hang about his neck or expect him to dance attendance on you all the time,' Kate said practically. 'Fortunately, you aren't madly in love with him so you won't want to cling ... and you won't make a fuss when he gets restless as every man does after a while. Leopards don't change their spots and Max is bound to amuse himself with other women occasionally. But those little affairs don't have to mean very much and they won't be any threat to you unless you allow them to be, you know ... and I'm sure you're too sensible for that!'

Abigail stared at her cousin in astonishment. 'Is that your recommended recipe for a happy marriage?'

'A successful marriage, anyway,' Kate amended, smiling. 'Make Max the kind of wife he wants and he won't wish to be rid of you— and you may have a very comfortable existence as Lady Constantine. Max won't object to what you do as long as you're discreet, you know. You may have your own friends and your own pleasures ... and I daresay Max will prefer you to have a life of your own, Abby. He's a busy man with many interests and he may not have as much time as he might wish to spend with you. You'll be wise to bear that in mind, you know.'

'You make it all sound so ... so cold-blooded,' Abigail said slowly, with distaste.

Kate's tone was ironic: 'Well, you're going

11

to marry him in cold blood, aren't you?'

She folded her arms tightly across her breasts in an instinctive gesture of self-defence. 'No, I'm not! I won't marry him,' she said but her tone lacked conviction. For she knew just how impossible it was to back out at virtually the last moment. There were too many pressures on all sides and no one to help her escape and she did not have the necessary courage or resolution to create a scandal by admitting that she had made a mistake.

Everyone liked and admired Max and envied her. No one would understand or forgive her if she jilted him almost at the altar. Perhaps Kate was right. Perhaps it was only last-minute nerves. Perhaps she could be quite content as his wife even though Max did not love her and she did not love him. Such marriages were not so rare and they were often more successful than a romantic idealist like herself cared to believe.

'Just make the most of what you get out of your marriage and don't fret if it isn't perfect all the time,' Kate said lightly, just as if Abigail had not spoken. 'It never is perfect—and it never could be, in my opinion! You and Max are individuals and you have to learn to live together and like it, to adapt to each other without losing your own identities. It won't be easy but it helps to like each other. I'm not talking about love, Abby. Any fool can fall in love but it takes a clever woman with a lot of patience and understanding to turn the average man into a good husband,' she added cynically. She scooped up the lid of the dress box and fitted it on. 'Well, I'm away to do this hem, my child. I'll be here at ten in the morning to dress you ... and I don't want to find that all my efforts have been wasted! But I daresay you'll be thankful that I didn't encourage you in this foolish nonsense about not wanting to marry Max!' She kissed the air in the vague direction of Abigail's cheek and was gone...

Abigail heaved a sigh as the door closed on her cousin. It had been a mistake trying to make Kate understand the panic in her breast. For Kate, like everyone else, believed that she was exceptionally lucky to be marrying Max Constantine with his wealth and brilliance and undeniable charm.

She was fortunate, of course ... if it was fortune to be the chosen bride of a very wealthy man of thirty-four who was strikingly handsome, kind and attentive and considerate, innately courteous—and utterly impersonal.

For Abigail was abruptly aware of how little she really meant to Max ... and that was even more off-putting than the realisation of how little he meant to her!

CHAPTER TWO

Max looked down at his bride. She was extremely pale and there were slight smudges beneath her eyes which hinted at a sleepless night. She was very tense ... and she seemed so vulnerable that his heart contracted with concern.

She was too young, too virginal, much too good for him. What on earth was he about to take this girl-child for his wife when he had lived the kind of life that made him most unsuited to marriage with any woman?

Her hand was in his clasp ... such a fragile little hand, fluttering slightly like a trapped bird within his firm grasp. He gave it a slight and reassuring squeeze and was rewarded with a tremulous little smile. But he fancied that it was a dutiful rather than a spontaneous response—and she did not glance at him. He realised that she had not once met his eyes during the ceremony.

Tall and lean, as dark as she was fair, he stood by her side in the crowded church, looking very handsome in the formal morning suit of the bridegroom. His black hair, crisp and waving, was worn a little long and tight curls nestled at the nape of his neck. His eyes were dark and piercing ... eyes that could seem hard and cold and utterly ruthless or could

14

smile with a warmth that had won him too many hearts. Now they were very grave and a nerve throbbed in his lean cheek and he was paying scant attention to the remainder of the ritual that united two strangers in matrimony.

For suddenly they were strangers, Max thought grimly. He had known that something was wrong when he turned to welcome his bride as she came down the aisle towards him ... and realised that she came to him like a sacrificial lamb to the altar.

He had expected her to be nervous, even apprehensive, a little shy and self-conscious now that the actual moment of marriage had arrived. He had not expected a reluctant bride! But he had immediately sensed reluctance combined with resignation—and he knew he was not mistaken!

The stranger by his side was not the warm, willing girl who had agreed so happily to his proposal and entered so eagerly into all the wedding plans and appeared as impatient as himself to begin their life together. She had been happy and excited and glad to be marrying him! Now it was just as though the warm delight within her that had first attracted him had been switched off like a light. She was cold and distant and withdrawn—and this was the girl who gave so much of herself to living that spirits visibly rose when she entered a room.

What had happened? How had it happened?

It was not his imagination, he knew. He was a sensitive man and his understanding and swift perception and intelligent interpretation of human behaviour had all helped to make him the successful businessman that he was. Abigail had never concealed her thoughts and feelings from him and her natural, warm-hearted candour had enchanted him. But now he discovered that her inability to lie, to dissemble, to play a part could hurt as well as enchant.

She stood by his side and uttered her responses in a quiet but clear voice—and he knew as surely as if she said so that she did not wish to be his wife. But she had promised to marry him and she would not go back on that promise. So she had allowed herself to be arrayed in all her bridal finery, transported in the bridal car to the church, escorted down the aisle on her uncle's arm to stand at the altar and commit herself to a marriage that she did not want in her heart of hearts.

Max was suddenly angry. He was flooded with anger so fierce, so consuming, that it almost drove him from that beautiful, ancient church and his beautiful, youthful bride. But he had already placed the wide gold band on the third finger of her left hand ... a hand that had trembled and jerked frantically away before steadying and accepting the ring with all its symbolism. And the words that made them irrevocably man and wife were even now

16

being spoken...

The words echoed in Abigail's heart that was so heavy and fearful. She had lain awake all night, knowing that she must not marry Max without really knowing why it seemed such a betrayal of her hopes and dreams, fretting over ways and means of escape even while she knew that escape was impossible. She was not left alone for a single moment once the household stirred. She was coaxed to eat breakfast although food threatened to choke her. She was encouraged and advised and applauded and told all over again how very fortunate she was and what a wonderful future she had before her and how happy she would be with Max... and the words of protest and pleading died on her lips in the face of everyone's determination to marry her to Max Constantine whether she wanted it or not!

There were last-minute arrivals of close relatives. There was a little, quite unnecessary panic about flowers. There was a flurry and scurry of bridesmaids. Then the hairdresser arrived and the beautician and Kate came with the bridal gown and veil and almost before she knew it, Abigail was bathed and powdered and coiffured and dressed. Resigned to her fate, she waited for the bridal car with her kindly and benevolent uncle who told her that she was very pretty and a lucky girl and everyone was very pleased and proud ... exactly as he had when she was seven years old and showing off

17

the rosette she had won with her pony in a local gymkhana!

Shaking, tightly clutching the white satin prayer book with its spray of white roses, Abigail walked down the aisle towards the waiting Max—and if he had but smiled in tender reassurance everything might have been all right, after all. But he was unsmiling, regarding her with those dark eyes that seemed to be much too perceptive, putting out his hand to claim her with easy, careless confidence she had once admired but which suddenly seemed to offend her. He had made up his mind to marry her, come what may, and had not anticipated the least difficulty in doing so ... and here she was according to plan, standing at the altar by his side as though she had no mind or heart of her own in the matter!

She went through the ceremony like a dutiful bride, making all the right responses, but resentment was raging in her breast. For this was not the wedding she had planned in all her youthful, roseate dreams of love and happiness ... except in the outward trappings. The essential thing was missing—the right man! For Max did not resemble the ideal she had cherished and refused to consider unattainable and only briefly forgotten while infatuation blinded her to the truth.

What a fool she had been to rush into this marriage with a man she scarcely knew! What a fool to fancy herself in love with the handsome

18

face and easy charm of an experienced and unscrupulous rake! It was all her own fault, of course ... but it helped to lay the blame on Max's shoulders for he had surely known how easy it would be to sweep her into marriage with his practised charm and smooth tongue!

Trembling, despairing, she signed her maiden name for the last time ... and lifted her face to receive the first kiss from her newly-acquired husband. His lips merely brushed her own, so cold that they chilled her heart, and then he was swept aside by the buoyancy of the best man who claimed his reward for the excellence with which he had carried out his duty of ensuring the bridegroom's presence at the church.

Moments later, Abigail walked on her new husband's arm up the aisle, scarcely aware of the sea of smiling faces and the murmur of good wishes, a tremulous smile pinned to her mouth and tears she did not dare to shed sparkling on her lashes. All unknowingly, she looked a radiantly happy bride. Max, troubled to the very depths of his being and at a loss for the first time in his life, escorted his beautiful bride from the church quite unaware that he looked every inch the proud bridegroom.

The patient crowd who waited outside the church came to life as bride and groom appeared and there were oohs and aahs of admiration and appreciation for the happy couple ... the well known and much admired

Max Constantine, so handsome, so wealthy, so brilliant, and his strikingly lovely bride in the exquisite gown.

In the car, Max sat back with a feeling of relief. He glanced at his bride's stony expression ... and noticed the slim fingers plucking so nervously at the spray of roses on the prayer book. For the few minutes that it would take the car to reach the hotel where the wedding reception was to be held, they were alone—and he ought to try to bridge the chasm that yawned between them. She was so young, still unsure of herself in this world that he knew so well. She must have been under more strain than he realised all these weeks and perhaps the actual wedding day had arrived too soon and made too many demands on her taut emotions. Later, when they were really alone and able to relax and be at ease with each other, he might discover all his fears and anxieties to be groundless, merely inspired by Abigail's nervousness and his own desperate desire that nothing should sweep her out of his arms at the last moment.

Max was thirty-four years old and there had been many women in his life. He had never loved any woman ... but he had looked into Abigail's dark-blue eyes, such shining pools of innocence and integrity, and discovered that he wanted more from life than the endless pursuit of pleasure. He knew that she had much to offer and much to give and that she was perhaps the only woman in the world who could secure his restless heart and keep him content. All in a moment, he had decided to marry her. Her willingness to be wooed and won had made it easy for him. She was very young and inexperienced and it had been a simple matter to persuade her into this marriage ... and he gave her credit for not being influenced by his wealth and position.

He did not doubt that he had possessed a very useful ally in Abigail's mother who had made no secret of her delight in the match. If Abigail had experienced any doubts in the weeks between their engagement and the wedding day, he was very sure that Esme Carr would have hastened to reassure her and laugh them away and even chide her daughter for having them in the first place!

Max had a sudden mental image of the small but indomitable figure of his newly-acquired mother-in-law. She even frightened him a little, he thought wryly, and felt very sure that it would take more courage than Abigail probably possessed to defy her mother's determination that the marriage should take place. If she had known a change of heart and wanted to cry off it seemed very likely that Esme Carr would have sternly forbidden her to do so—and if that were the case then he must be torn between gratitude and acute dislike of the pressures put upon Abigail to marry him.

No man could wish for an unwilling bride,

after all. At the same time, honest with himself, he knew that he wanted Abigail on any terms! His longing for her was greater than anything he had ever experienced. But her youth, her innocence, her very trust had urged him to tread warily all these weeks. He had forced himself to be a light-hearted and undemanding lover and he doubted that she had the least inkling of the degree of desire that she inspired in him. Wanting her as he had never wanted any other woman in his life, Max had schooled himself to patience with a self-control he had been astonished to find that he possessed. But he had known that it was very important to impress upon Abigail that he regarded her in a very different light to all those other women in his past. For she was soon to be his wife—and no other woman had ever come near to attaining that position!

Abigail's heart was swelling with anger and pride and chagrin. How little it all meant to him! How easy it was for him to sit back with a smile of satisfaction now that he had what he wanted! How little he must care for her if he could not sense the ordeal it had been for her and how miserable she felt at this very moment—and how thankful she was that he did not realise how little she wanted to be his wife! She had married him for better or worse—and it would never do for him to know that she already felt it was the worst thing that could have happened to her!

22

The silence was oppressive. It seemed that he did not mean to break it—so she must. She forced a smile to stiff lips. 'I expect you're thankful that part is over,' she said as brightly as she could. 'Men don't really like the business of getting married, do they? But everything went off very well, don't you think?'

He noticed that the smile did not reach her eyes. She was uttering polite nothings, he thought wearily. Was she so shy, so ill at ease—or was she merely intent on keeping him at arms' length for as long as possible? He ached to sweep her into his arms but this was scarcely the time nor the place ... and he admitted wryly that he was afraid of a rebuff. It was astonishing that a man with all his knowledge and experience of women should be so much at a loss in his dealings with this one!

'Superb organisation on somebody's part,' he said lightly, deciding to play his part in the charade if that was what she wanted.

'Oh, not mine,' she disclaimed quickly. 'I had very little to do with all the arrangements, you know.'

'Your mother is a wonderful woman,' he said, a little drily. A wry smile flickered about his mouth. Without looking at his bride, he went on with seeming flippancy: 'I wonder if you'd have married me at all if she hadn't been so determined to have me for a son-in-law!'

Panic caught her by the throat. He knew! It was impossible but he knew just how

23

reluctantly she had walked down that aisle to marry him! Those dark eyes had looked right into her heart and mind, just as she had feared!

Suddenly Abigail knew that she was afraid of him. He could be hard and ruthless, even cruel—everyone said so. He was a very proud man and no one hurt or humiliated him without paying the penalty. He was not likely to forgive a wife who admitted to any regrets about marrying him ... and although she could not think of any punishment he could inflict that might be worse than being married to a man she did not love in the least, she was still afraid to tell him the truth.

The vows were made and they must be kept—no matter what it cost her! And she must say and do everything that was necessary to convince him of her happiness ... although it might mean lying and deceiving and playing a part when such things were so alien to her nature.

Heaven knew how she managed that light laugh—but she did! 'Mama wasn't standing behind me when I agreed to marry you, Max,' she said, marvelling at the lightness of her tone and the promptness of her response. 'Naturally she is very pleased about it but I chose you for myself.' She leaned forward to touch her lips briefly to his lean cheek. 'No one twisted my arm, Max!' It was true. She had wanted to marry him ... until she had woken out of that foolish dream less than twenty-four hours ago!

24

And no one could have forced her to go through with the ceremony—and no one would have wanted to force her however disappointed they might be, she told herself fairly. It was her own realisation of the impossibility of backing out at the last minute and exposing Max and herself to the gossip and speculation that would be rife that had taken her to the church that day. It was her own fault for realising too late that she did not love him ... but if Kate was to be believed quite a few successful marriages were founded on a lot less than love.

Max felt his heart lighten as he caught a brief glimpse of the Abigail who had swept away all his dislike of losing his freedom. He was very ready to believe her sincere and he reached for her hand and carried it to his lips. 'You're so sweet,' he said quietly. 'I hope you are going to be happy with me, Abigail.'

As the car began to slow its approach to the hotel, she drew away her hand and began to gather up her long train in readiness to alight and it gave her sufficient excuse to avoid his dark eyes. 'Of course I shall,' she exclaimed brightly and with more conviction than she really felt. 'I shall have everything a woman could want, after all...'

The champagne flowed—and so did the line of guests. Abigail was astonished to discover that she had so many relatives, old and new; so many friends and acquaintances to wish her

25

happy and congratulate Max on his good fortune. There was no time for introspective thought and she was almost thankful that they were leaving early for their honeymoon although she refused to dwell on what lay before her once she was really alone with the man she had married.

Surrounded by a trio of laughing, envious girlfriends, Abigail did not know what made her turn round suddenly, eagerly, her heart lifting in strange anticipation ... until she saw Toby. Her heart seemed to stop and then it plunged into warm, flowing vibrancy and she held out both hands to him with so much eager delight in her dark-blue eyes that Max, coming to claim his bride and remind her of the time, was checked in his approach, his own eyes narrowing with swift and painful suspicion...

CHAPTER THREE

Toby smiled ... the lazy, enchanting smile that had captured her heart when she was seven and he was almost a man of twelve. Abigail clung to his strong, familiar hands and gazed up into the mischievous blue eyes that teased her gently for betraying feelings she could never hide where he was concerned.

Toby! Her first and only and lasting love! He smiled down at her with unmistakable affection mingled with gentle reproach and she knew that he reminded her of the pact they had made as children and renewed whenever they met throughout the years—the pact to marry each other one day!

She had not really forgotten. How could she forget anyone so dear, so precious, so much a part of her life? How could she forget a promise that she had cherished for so many years? But Max had walked into her life and banished the dream for a few brief weeks with his almost hypnotic charm and his undeniable powers of persuasion.

It was over a year since she had seen Toby. He was an actor and he had been in America making a name for himself in films in recent years and she had seen him on a flying visit. He was a careless correspondent, failing to answer most of her letters. It had been easy to dismiss his claim to her affection as child's play while she was so flattered and so excited by Max's attentions. But now she knew that it had been much more than a childhood game of let's pretend throughout the years. She had supposed that Toby was far from her mind and heart but in truth he had never really left either, she realised. Her uneasiness as her wedding to another man drew near had been born of the instinctive knowledge that it was impossible for her to love anyone but Toby ... and now he was here in person to remind her of their lasting need of each other.

27

He held her hands very tightly, smiling into her eyes—and then he stooped to kiss her, claiming the right of a cousin. Abigail caught her breath as their lips met and knew that she loved him, had always loved him, could never cease to love him.

'Toby...' she said, as she had already said three times, his name an endearment on her lips.

'Darling Abby,' he said easily. 'I always told you that you would be a very beautiful bride.' His tone was light and the words were the kind of remark that any affectionate cousin might utter. But they stabbed her with the sense of all that she had lost and the terrible thing that she had done ... and she knew that he reproached her. He was very angry and so bitter that he would never forgive her, she thought bleakly. She had broken their pact. She had not waited. She had failed to trust him...

'But you're in America,' she said foolishly when she could manage to say something more than his name.

He nodded. 'So I am ... while you're getting married behind my back. I thought I was meant to play a prominent part at your wedding and I end up as just another guest. It's too bad of you, Abby!' He was smiling—and only Abigail knew the anger behind the smile, the bitterness behind the words.

'I never thought ... I didn't dare to hope—oh, Toby, I'm so *glad* to see you!' she

28

exclaimed joyfully, her heart in eyes and voice, not caring that the whole world might recognise his importance to her. 'You're staying over here now? You won't go away again?' she demanded anxiously. 'Oh, Toby, I have missed you!'

It was a cry from the heart and his hands tightened convulsively on her slender fingers. 'I guess I stayed away too long,' he said, a little wry. They talked for a moment or two, eagerly, like lovers meeting after long separation, and Abigail was blind and deaf to everything but his presence. Then he turned away, leaving her abruptly, as Max came towards them … and she knew that he could not face an introduction to the man that she had married. She looked after him in anguish, suddenly realising what she had done…

She looked a lost child in the swirling crowd—small, slight, ridiculously young, much too pale, eyes enormous in a suddenly pinched face. Max felt a surge of protective tenderness. Reaching her, he put an arm about the slender waist and drew her close with smiling reassurance in his dark eyes. But there was unconscious resistance in her taut body and her gaze was upon the tall man who was already flirting with one of the bridesmaids. His eyes darkened. He wanted to seize her in his arms and carry her off … away from the danger that he sensed in her interest in the other man. But he was too shrewd, too mature,

29

too level-headed to betray that he had closely observed and much disliked that brief encounter.

Deliberately he followed her gaze and said lightly: 'I believe I know that face. Friend or family, darling?'

'Oh ... family!' she said, her heart jumping. 'A cousin of mine ... Toby—Toby Joslin. I don't think you know him. You may have seen one of his films. He's doing very well in America. I ... I had no idea he would be over here for the wedding,' she went on stammering slightly although there was nothing in his manner to unnerve her. He appeared to evince a very natural interest in a member of her family. 'It ... it was such a surprise to see him,' she added in rather lame explanation of the glowing delight that he might have observed.

Max wondered when she had discovered that cousin Toby was in England—and was abruptly sure that the discovery had effectively banished all her desire for their marriage. 'You're fond of him,' he commented carefully.

There was nothing in the dark eyes to account for her sudden uneasiness. She decided wryly that it was simply an attack of guilt. It was most unlikely that Max would be jealous of Toby or any man she chose to encourage. He was much too sure of himself to be unsure of her, she thought drily. It would not occur to Max Constantine, darling of society, that a woman found it impossible to love and want him!

'Yes—oh yes!' she said brightly. 'I've known him all my life.' Had loved him all her life, she might have added! 'We're great friends, Max. You must meet him when we get back from honeymoon—if he's still in England. And you won't mind if I see something of him when you are busy, will you?' she added with careful carelessness.

He would mind, he thought grimly. He would mind very much. The last thing he wanted was a man from her past dancing attendance on her and filling her head and heart with romantic nonsense! Now he knew why she had come like a lamb to the slaughter instead of a radiant and triumphant bride to her wedding. Now he knew why she seemed so detached, so remote. If only he knew why she had chosen to go through with their marriage when she was so obviously in love with another man!

Again that fierce anger swept over him. For a moment, a red mist swam before his eyes and he would happily have felled her cousin Toby with a sledge-hammer if one had been conveniently at hand.

He was not given to such rages and it appalled him that Abigail had so much power over his emotions and could inspire such violence. It was anger born of fear, he knew... the dread of losing her walked hand in hand with the delight of loving her.

31

With a considerable effort, he controlled his fury and forced himself to assure her lightly that she might do just as she wished and see her friends or any member of her family as often as she chose. With admirable restraint, he did not add that he hoped she would have more regard for his feelings and her reputation than to run around town in the company of her good-looking cousin. He realised only too well that she was indifferent to his feelings. She was only concerned with her own and she was quite young enough to suppose that regard for one's reputation was old-fashioned, he thought wryly...

A day had never seemed so long. At the same time, it was much too soon that Abigail found herself entirely alone with her husband. Now she really had to face the fact that they were married. It was foolish to be so apprehensive. Max was not an ogre, after all. But she shrank instinctively from the very thought of his lovemaking. At the back of her mind was the constant image of Toby's dear face—the dancing blue eyes, the whimsical quirk to his smile, the slight cleft in his chin and the boyish fall of thick fair hair across his brow. They shared so many memories, she thought wistfully, remembering. He was so dear, so familiar, so precious a part of her life. She ached for him and her heart throbbed with love for him and tears tugged at her throat as she realised the futility of loving and wanting him

32

now that she had so foolishly married Max.

She leaned against the stone balustrade of the terrace with its steps leading down to the beach. It was growing dark and stars were beginning to twinkle against the deepening velvet of the sky. She was desperately tired but she would not admit to it and she had kept up a light barrage of conversation and laughter during the drive to the airport and the flight across the channel and the short journey to Max's villa on the Cote d'Azur. It had been her own choice for their honeymoon but now she wished with all her heart that they had stayed in London so that she might snatch the occasional meeting with Toby.

Max had not been deceived by the gaiety and exuberance of her mood and he perfectly understood her wish to linger over drinks on the terrace. But his desire was growing and his patience was running out, he thought a little grimly. Her head might be full of her cousin just now but he would give her something else to think about ... and he doubted if her youthful dream would survive the reality of marriage with a man who could really teach her the meaning of love.

Swirling the brandy in his glass, he studied his beautiful bride in the apricot trouser suit she had worn for travelling. Her shining hair lay in a thick coil over one shapely breast. He drank the brandy and set down the glass and rose to his feet in one decisive movement ...

33

and Abigail's heartbeat quickened in sudden trepidation.

She smiled at him, nervously. 'I love it here,' she said brightly. 'It's so beautiful. I could stay and watch the sea all night.'

He put a hand to the long tress of her hair and twined his fingers through the silken strands. He smiled down at her with warm intent in his dark eyes. 'You are beautiful,' he said softly, his voice low and caressing and heavy with desire. He bent his head to touch her lips lightly with his own, drawing her close with an arm about her slender waist. 'Come to bed,' he murmured with sudden, throbbing urgency. 'The sea will still be here in the morning...'

She was tense, trembling. Max forced down the impatience that rose in him. He wanted her so much but he must be patient, gentle, understanding—and he did not want her at all if she came unwillingly to his arms, he thought on a surge of angry pain.

Abigail's lips were dry and her mind was revolving in panic and her body shrank from the very touch of his hand. Desperately, she reminded herself that she had known he would inevitably make demands on her as soon as they were married despite the lack of interest he had shown during their engagement. No doubt there had been other women to satisfy his needs then, she thought wryly ... and now there was only herself.

She was under no illusions about the man she had married. Too many people had gone out of their way to emphasise his reputation as a womaniser for her to doubt that he was a sensual man with strong sexual appetites—and it had piqued her femininity that he seemed so indifferent to her attractions although he wished to marry her. It had added fuel to the belief that he married her for other reasons than the usual ones! She was young and healthy and of excellent family and he wanted an heir ... and she supposed it did not matter that she lacked the experience that a man like Max wanted in a woman.

It was difficult to believe that once she had thrilled to the thought of his lovemaking when they were married and even resented his insistence on treating her with patient and gentle courtesy. But then she had thought him attractive and exciting and his kiss had stirred the dormant delight in the depths of her being. Now, hugging the thought of Toby to her heart, she wondered how she could endure this man's embrace without betraying instinctive revulsion.

'Give me ten minutes,' she said as lightly as she could. She managed a slight smile and went into the house, telling herself desperately that there was no reason to be afraid for Max was kind and considerate and he would understand her shyness and apprehension and make everything easy for her.

35

Well-trained staff had melted discreetly away to their own quarters. A maid had unpacked for Abigail and the filmy chiffon nightgown and matching negligee lay across the wide bed. Abigail closed the bedroom door and stood with her back against it, her heart thumping heavily in her breast. The bed seemed to dominate the room. The tensions of the day had given her a headache and she felt slightly sick. Perhaps she was coming down with 'flu, she thought hopefully—and decided ruefully that not even a raging temperature would keep a determined man from claiming his bride. She sensed that Max was very determined. Slowly she began to unfasten the buttons of her silk suit...

She stood by the window in the loose flowing nightgown, newly-brushed hair falling about her slender shoulders, waiting for Max. It was surely more than ten minutes since she had left him, she thought with impatience. He must know her state of mind and how anxious she was to have an end to this ordeal of a wedding night, she thought crossly.

She turned, starting, as the door opened— and Max frowned, disliking the look of the trapped animal in her eyes. He supposed it was too much to expect her to greet him with smiling eagerness and outstretched arms! Yet only days before he would have placed bets on her willingness to welcome him into her bed! He cursed Toby Joslin to hell and beyond—

36

and moved swiftly to take her into his arms and capture her reluctant mouth.

His kiss was urgent, demanding. His arms were strong and compelling and his body was tense with the desire that he had restrained for too long. She resisted him and anger flared and he caught her up into his arms and swept her to the bed in sudden resolution. He took her swiftly, fiercely—and Abigail, powerless in the strength of his embrace, lay in his arms, hating him.

She was silent, totally unresponsive, enduring rather than enjoying the brief intimacy. Spent, Max groaned in dismay and touched his lips to the frail, pulsing hollow of her throat. He was angry, dejected, utterly disappointed, hurt to the very heart of him by her rejection. So much for the great lover, he mocked himself in disgust. He had been as impatient and inconsiderate and selfish as any callow youth with his first woman ... and he had meant this first time with Abigail to be very precious, very meaningful for them both! 'Oh, Abby...' he said wryly. 'That isn't the way it was meant to be.'

Angry, humiliated, oddly filled with bitter disappointment, she jerked from him. 'Don't call me that!' she said coldly, fiercely, feeling that the tenderness of the pet name was sadly out of place between them. 'I hate it!' It was as near as she dared to declaring that she hated him.

37

Max sat up and reached for his robe, seeking the cigarettes and lighter that he had placed in the pocket. His heart was very heavy. He had hoped to coax Abigail into loving him with the tender delight they would find in each other's arms. Now he was sure that he had driven her even further from loving him at all ... and he wondered if he would ever be able to redeem the disastrous beginning to their marriage. With any other woman it would not have mattered—but with any other it would never have happened, he thought wryly. He loved her too much and longed too greatly for the love of the only woman who had really meant anything to him.

'Please don't smoke!' Abigail said sharply. 'I can't bear the smell of tobacco in my bedroom!' Utterly desolate and chilled by despair, she pulled the covers closely about her nakedness and with her face carefully averted she allowed the slow and painful tears to trickle down her cheeks to dampen the pillow. So much for all her innocent dreams of their wedding night, she thought bleakly, bitterly.

'Sorry ...' Max was instantly contrite, eager to please in even the smallest way. He returned the cigarette to the pack and tossed both pack and lighter on to the table beside the bed. The tension in her still body tugged at his heart and he turned to her, put an arm over her and tried to coax her to turn her face towards him with light fingers beneath her chin. He heard the

38

swift, impatient catch of her breath before she jerked away from his touch. He sighed. 'Don't be angry, Abigail,' he said softly.

'You hurt me,' she said coldly—and could not explain even to herself why the hurt had been so much more than physical.

'Darling!' He drew her swiftly, strongly into his arms, forcing her to turn. 'Forgive me ... kiss me, Abigail!' He looked into the swimming pools of dark blue and there was tender regret in his own eyes. Because she ignored his plea, he kissed her, light butterfly kisses that traced a path from unresponsive mouth to soft hair and back again. 'I didn't mean to hurt you, sweetheart,' he said with a note in his voice that no other woman had ever heard.

Abigail lay in his arms, listening to the endearments that seemed so empty, accepting the kisses that were mere tokens of apology, longing and longing for Toby until she felt her swelling heart must break. And in his arms, she eventually fell asleep with tears wet on her long lashes, emotionally and physically exhausted—and Max held her close against his heart, loving her so much that it hurt, fearing that she would never love him, sensing that all her thoughts and feelings were tied up in another man even while she lay with him and knowing that it had been a mistake to marry her. He had reached out with both hands for the happiness that she seemed to promise but he was desperately afraid that it might always

39

elude him, after all...

CHAPTER FOUR

With the dawn, Abigail was suddenly conscious of his nearness. She had slept heavily, dreamlessly and scarcely knew what had woken her. She lifted herself carefully on to her elbow and regarded the sleeping man by her side in the early light of the morning. He was very good-looking. He looked younger than his thirty-four years, she thought in surprise.

Remembering the lovemaking that had seemed more of an assault than the ecstatic experience she had been led to expect, she was flooded with revulsion and resentment. As he moved slightly in his sleep, her body instinctively tensed to avoid any physical contact with him. She could not bear the thought of his touch and she shuddered at the memory of the ruthless disregard for anything but his own desire and its gratification. She felt used, abused ... and suddenly determined that it should not happen again. He would not possess her again by force or any other means, she thought fiercely, resentfully. She did not care what damage she did to their relationship because of her attitude. Their marriage was ruined before it had ever begun! She wished it were possible to wave a magic wand and transport herself back to the previous morning. For nothing on earth would have taken her to that church to marry Max if she had known what marriage to him would mean!

She was his wife and she would do everything that was expected of her ... except sleep with him! If he objected then she would remind him that he only had himself to blame. Why, it had been little more than rape! He was utterly despicable and she would never forgive him ...

Max woke, wondering why he felt so heavy of heart, so utterly low in spirits ... and then remembered. With renewed contrition, he put out a hand to Abigail ... and discovered that he was alone in the big bed. He rolled over to look at his watch. It was seven o'clock and the birds were singing and the sun was shining and he was on his honeymoon with the woman he loved ... and heaven knew where she was!

He threw back the light covers and reached for his robe. 'Abigail ...!' he called. He knocked lightly on the door that led into the adjoining bathroom. 'Abigail!' Tentatively he opened the door. The room was empty but there were signs that it had recently been used and the perfume of bath salts lingered on the air.

Max strode to the window and stepped out to the little balcony. There was no sign of Abigail on the terrace below or on the beach beyond. Perhaps it was foolish to feel the beginning of panic ... but he showered and shaved and dressed in record time and ran down to look for his wife.

At last, he found her in the garden. She looked fresh and lovely and clear-eyed in the morning sunlight. She wore beige trousers and shirt and her hair was tucked into a matching turban and there was a new maturity and assurance about her as she greeted him. She moved towards him, cool and quite composed, and Max discovered that the warm and loving words that had trembled on his lips were silenced by the sudden knowledge that she had no wish to hear them. She was determined not to love him and she did not want him to love her, he realised with a sinking heart.

'I've been looking for you,' he told her, his tone a little harsh with ridiculous relief. He had not really thought her gone, run from him in the middle of the night, and yet he had feared the possibility of it!

'I've been for a walk,' she said carelessly. 'I like to walk in the early morning. It's the best time of the day. I didn't expect you to be up and about so early. I think it's too soon for breakfast but I expect I can organise some coffee.'

'Good idea,' he said, rather at a loss in the face of her brisk efficiency. This was an Abigail he did not know, he thought a little wryly. She had always been rather diffident, certainly shy,

42

a gentle, lovable and very appealing girl. He did not know that he welcomed the change that made her seem a carbon copy of her indomitable mother. Was it simply a part of her character that she had kept concealed until they were safely married? Or was it all part and parcel of the very natural anger and resentment that he had inspired with his callow handling of his virgin bride.

They drank coffee on the terrace. She dealt with the coffee-pot and the delicate cups with graceful economy of movement and Max knew that it would always delight him to watch her at such times.

'What would you like to do today?' he asked carefully, stirring his coffee.

'Oh, just laze, I think,' she said coolly. 'Everything has been so hectic for so long that it will be delightful to do nothing. How about you?'

'Whatever pleases you, Abigail.' He smiled at her with warmth. 'It's your honeymoon, darling.' He saw that she winced away from the word and there was no answering smile in her eyes. He reached to cover the hand that lay on the table with his own. She tensed, enduring his touch without the slightest pleasure in it—and Max knew that she only endured. How little she cared for him, he thought with bitterness sweeping into his heart. 'You are miles away from me,' he said quietly, wondering why she had married him and if their marriage could

43

ever hope to succeed when there was such a gulf between his feelings and hers.

Abigail rose and went to stand by the stone balustrade of the terrace, taking her coffee cup with her. 'The sea is very inviting. I think I shall swim before breakfast,' she said as though he had not spoken. She felt utterly indifferent to him. The loathing and resentment of first awakening had given way to cold contempt. She would play the necessary part of wife as far as she was able, having married him, but he need not expect her to be warm and loving and intent on pleasing him, she thought coldly. He had not treated her with any warmth or tenderness and pleasing her had certainly been the last thing in his mind!

Determined not to be treated as a stranger by his own wife, Max rose and went to her side. He touched his fingers to her soft cheek in a light caress and was ridiculously pleased that she did not flinch away as he had half-expected. 'You're very energetic,' he said, teasing her. 'Walking, swimming—all before breakfast! You'll leave an old man like me way behind, I'm afraid.'

'There's no need for you to come with me,' she said carelessly, her tone leaving him in no doubt that she did not want him. 'I'm a very strong swimmer. I shall be perfectly safe on my own.' She carried her coffee cup back to the table in order to escape his nearness. She might be very young and very inexperienced but she was quite capable of sensing desire in a man. Unless she kept him firmly at arms' length it seemed very likely that the moment she really dreaded would be on her before she had carefully rehearsed all she meant to say to him. It was not going to be easy to tell him of her decision . . . but it must be preferable to more of the lovemaking that had left her bruised in mind and body.

Max was much too proud to betray his hurt or to force his company where it was not wanted. If she chose to punish him in a rather childish way for the urgency and impatience that a man as much in love as himself had been quite unable to help then there was very little he could do about it, he thought wryly. He was prepared to make every allowance for her youth and her sensitivity and he was determined to do all he could to atone for the disappointment and disillusion she had known. She did not realise that his disappointment had been much greater than her own, of course. Because he loved, he had wanted it to be a perfect experience for them both. But he comforted himself with the thought that their honeymoon had only just begun and soon she would recover from her pique and be his sweet and enchanting and wholly delightful Abigail once more . . . and the next time that she lay in his arms he would not allow his emotions to run away with him!

She maintained her coolness throughout the

45

day ... and Max managed to retain his temper despite the deliberate provocation in her attitude to him. She rebuffed him at every turn ... lightly but quite unmistakenly. He simply could not get close to her, mentally or physically. She had closed her mind and heart to him and her body seemed to shrink from his merest touch. The woman he loved so dearly and had believed that he knew so well had become an impersonal stranger.

He continued to make allowances. She was tired. She was suffering from a very natural reaction after the weeks of anticipation and preparation. She was finding it difficult to adjust to being entirely alone with him in this quiet and secluded place when they had always been surrounded by people and the hustle and bustle of town life. She was shy and not very sure of herself in unfamiliar surroundings. Perhaps it had been a mistake to whisk her off to the South of France but it had been Abigail's own wish and it hurt him to recall how happily she had anticipated these days when they would be together as man and wife for the first time. But that had been before the abrupt change of heart that he could only attribute to her cousin Toby.

He had not even known of the man's existence which seemed a little surprising if she was so very fond of him and they had virtually grown up together as brother and sister, he thought drily, recalling that she had been

46

anxious to impress him with the innocence in their association. He could not rid himself of a mental image of his beautiful bride with her hands in another man's clasp and her eyes glowing with delight and her whole being alive with emotions that the man obviously inspired.

Max did not want to accept that Abigail was in love with her cousin. But she was certainly not in love with him and he refused to dwell on the reasons she might have had for marrying him in cold blood. He would not believe that she had simply wanted to be Lady Constantine with all the attendant advantages. He would not believe that she had been pressured by an ambitious mother into accepting him. He preferred to believe that she had known herself on the threshold of loving him until cousin Toby came back into her life to fill her with doubts and hesitations when it seemed too late to cancel the wedding arrangements. If she had been near to loving him then his case could not be so hopeless, he told himself optimistically.

Her feelings for Toby Joslin might be just a hangover from an adolescent infatuation. He might be making too much of a very ordinary affection between cousins. However it was, he had one essential advantage over the other man—Abigail was his wife! If she did not love him then it was up to him to coax her into loving him ... and surely that was not so impossible for a man with all his experience of women! The first essential was patience and he

47

would need much of that, he thought wryly. For Abigail was not the demure and diffident and delightful bride he had expected. Indifference lent self-assurance and a confidence that was disconcerting...

Curled up on a couch, listening with only half an ear to the music from the stereo, Abigail was growing sleepier with every moment. It had been a long and difficult day and she was longing to go to bed but nothing would induce her to admit to it. A yawn took her by surprise and she stifled it swiftly with an apprehensive glance at Max.

He smiled at her with easy warmth and leaned forward to crush his cigar into the ashtray. 'Swimming and sunbathing and doing nothing all day makes one ridiculously weary,' he said lightly. 'I don't know about you, darling, but I'm very ready to tumble into bed.'

Steeling herself, she said tautly: 'Sleep in the guest room, will you, Max? I don't want you with me. I'm tired and you'll disturb me too much. I scarcely slept at all last night.'

He heard her out without a flicker of expression in his dark eyes. Then he said carelessly: 'Just as you wish, Abigail.' He rose and walked over to the stereo to take off the record as it finished and then placed it carefully in its sleeve.

Abigail waited for him to say something more, to reproach her, to plead with her perhaps. She glanced at him and saw that he was quite unconcerned ... and she got up from the couch and walked towards the door, oddly irritated by his calm acceptance of her suggestion. 'Goodnight then, Max,' she said brightly, pausing by the door to give him one more chance of protest.

He did not turn. 'Goodnight, my dear.'

The door closed with a little snap. Max put a hand to his ear and pulled gently at the lobe, an unconscious habit when he was deeply disturbed. He was hurt and angry but not at all surprised. He had been waiting for Abigail to say something of the kind for she had been at pains to keep him at even more of a distance throughout the evening.

With the coming of night she had grown more apprehensive. He wondered if she was still set on punishing him or if she merely dreaded a repetition of lovemaking that she had found so very unsatisfactory. He supposed she would not tell him, whichever it was!

Long after she was in bed, Abigail heard him moving about in the adjoining room. No doubt he thought her fast asleep, she thought, marvelling at that calm acceptance of the situation. Or was he so calm? He certainly seemed to be very restless—because he wanted her or because he was very angry with her, she wondered curiously. Her rejection of him must surely have seemed like a slap in the face to a man like Max.

It was ridiculous to feel so guilty. But she

49

was his wife, after all. She supposed he had certain rights that she ought not to deny him. But much more than that, no one liked to be rejected and rebuffed even if they deserved it. Had she hurt him? She knew how she would feel if she stood in his shoes! She had been rather unkind to him all day, she realised on a surge of conscience—and he had taken it all without anger or resentment. She wondered if she ought to call him into the room, say sorry, hold out her arms to him and give him a chance to prove that he was not the sensual, selfish, insensitive brute he had seemed on the previous night.

Abigail thought of his warm lips against the hollow of her throat and the strength of his arms about her and the urgency in his embrace ... and a tiny shudder ran through her slight body. Abruptly rejecting a strange weakness that she would certainly regret, she buried her head in the pillows and resolutely determined on sleep...

Max could not sleep. He mixed himself another drink, smoked a last cigar, read a few pages of a book without taking in a single word, stood on the balcony and stared out to sea and thought of the wide world beyond and all the women in it and the many women he had known and lightly loved ... and knew that for the rest of his life there would only be one woman in his world.

Eventually he climbed into the empty bed

50

and switched off the light. He lay on his back in the clinging darkness and still could not sleep. It was not only that he was so conscious of his lovely and eminently desirable wife sleeping in the next room. Certainly his arms ached to hold her close and his body throbbed with desire and his heart yearned for the sweet warmth of the affection she had so generously bestowed on him until they were actually married. But his heart and mind were much more troubled than his body. He was bewildered and hurt and deeply disappointed and yet he was very ready to forgive and forget. He loved her very much. He would endure anything to keep her by his side. There would be no word of reproach, no hint of resentment. When she was ready she would come to him . . . until then he would be patient, resigned, understanding.

Abigail did not love him and she was not the sort of woman who could give herself without love, he realised. He understood. He would accept. He would live with her as brother and sister if it would please her, reassure her, make her happy. He would not ask anything of her that she was not glad to give, he resolved . . . but for all the nobility and integrity of his resolution, his heart was very heavy.

CHAPTER FIVE

Max returned from a solitary walk along the shore to find Abigail on the terrace, sunbathing in the skimpiest of bikinis, her hair pinned in a careless, tumbling knot on top of her head. Her lovely body was already a glorious golden-brown after long hours of lazing in the sun.

At the sound of his step, she sat up, reaching for a short towelling robe and drawing it about her near-nudity. His jaw tensed. Following on everything else, the gesture seemed to be deliberately offensive. He was a patient man but his patience had been sorely tried in the last few days, he thought grimly. He had forgiven much but that seemed to be the last straw.

He had intended to greet her with warm friendliness in yet one more attempt to bridge the chasm that yawned between them consistently but with the bitterness of gall rising in his throat, he said tersely: 'Oh, don't cover up! The sight of your body won't make me throw myself on you with lustful intent. I can live without the kind of rebuffs that you hand out, Abigail.'

The colour rushed into her face. It was not surprising that he should be so sensitive but she had not meant to offend him. Purely by chance, she had reached for her robe just as he mounted the stone steps to the terrace. But there was some justification for his resentment, she supposed. It was the first time she had worn the very brief bikini and she did feel a little self-conscious and he might easily have sensed her embarrassment and a desire to cover up. She was very shy with him still.

'It's time for lunch,' she said stiffly, a little defensively. 'I'm just going in to change.'

Max glanced at his watch. 'Lunch! Where has the morning gone? Time flies when one is enjoying life, doesn't it?'

Abigail decided to ignore the goading irony in the words. He was angry because she had refused to walk with him on the plea that she wanted to sunbathe before the sun became too hot for comfort. He was even angrier that they had slept apart since that first night, she supposed. They did not talk about it. There was merely acceptance, silent and understood, that she did not want his lovemaking and meant to avoid it by sleeping alone.

But he could not like it, she realised. He was a proud man and her dislike of his embrace must strike deeply at his ego. But she could not believe that it really mattered very much to him, otherwise. After all, it was three days since he had attempted even the merest touch of her hand—and that was scarcely the behaviour of an ardent and loving man. If he cared for her at all, really wanted her, he would surely be trying to persuade her into his arms!

He was courteous and charming and

53

pleasant, much more attentive than she probably deserved, she thought a little wryly. He spent all his time in trying to please her, in doing what she wanted, in taking her out and about so that they were seldom on their own at the villa. But there was nothing of the lover in his manner ... any more than there had been during their engagement, she recalled. It seemed to Abigail that she simply did not attract him physically. He had probably carried out a bridegroom's duty without a trace of real feeling for her—and in retrospect it seemed the behaviour of a man who regarded his bride with distaste but knew that the marriage must be consummated.

Of course, she had always known that he did not love her but she had been too infatuated to question his wish to marry her, she thought bitterly.

It could only be a marriage of convenience for Max. He wanted a son and he had decided that she would do very well as his wife—and she had been willing enough to marry him, she recalled ruefully. But while they lived together as strangers it was not likely that he would get the son he wanted. At the moment he probably did not feel that the matter was urgent. But eventually he must expect her to oblige him— and she would have to relent if their marriage was to succeed at all!

She gathered up the impedimenta of oils, creams and tissues and went into the house to dress. Max, pouring himself a drink, looked after her with something akin to dislike in his heart. Instantly, he was repentant. How could he be angry, resentful, when he loved her no matter what she did or said to hurt and disappoint him!

Abigail's long, silky hair tumbled about her shoulders as she took out the pins. She reached for the brush that stood on the dressing-table—and checked in dismay as she saw Max reflected in the mirror. He stood just inside the door that she had not heard open and there was a smiling warmth in his dark eyes that she immediately interpreted as intent. With a little catch of her breath, she turned to face him, defiant and defensive, her hand instinctively tightening on the hair-brush.

Amusement quirked at the corner of his mouth.

'Are you about to throw that at me?' he asked lightly.

'Don't make it necessary,' she warned.

He went towards her in deliberate provocation, far from being as amused as he seemed. In fact, he was extremely irritated by her attitude.

Her heart quickened with apprehension. 'Don't touch me, Max!' she exclaimed involuntarily.

His smile vanished. 'Good God, Abigail!' he said, suddenly impatient. 'Let's have an end to this nonsense!' He took the brush from her

55

hand and tossed it carelessly on to the dressing-table. She backed away and he reached for her angrily with a relentless hand on her shoulder, drew her towards him and kissed her almost roughly. He had yearned for her all the week. Suddenly his need for her was greater than all his resolution to be patient, tolerant, understanding. Love moved strongly in him and he kissed her with a fierce, demanding impatience with the folly that had kept her from his arms too long...

His hand was firmly entwined in the long strands of her hair. Abigail struggled to escape from his kiss and only succeeded in bringing tears to her eyes as her hair was pulled. Her hands were on his chest and she exerted all her strength in the endeavour to push him away, her breast heaving with the tumult of her emotions. She would not be taken again in cold blood, she thought fiercely, sensing only the desire in his embrace and quite insensitive to the love and the need behind it.

Abruptly he released her ... and she staggered, losing her balance. He regarded her coldly. Abigail put her hands to her hair and swept it back from her stormy face. 'Oh, I hate you!' she declared fiercely, intensely.

A nerve throbbed in his cheek. 'That's a lot of hate,' he said quietly, the pain of rejection flooding him to the point of despair. 'I wish I knew how I've earned it.' He pulled gently at the lobe of his ear, a frown in his dark eyes.

'What did I do, Abigail?'

She sat down at the dressing-table and picked up the brush. She pulled it through her tangled hair with a hand that shook, needing to be doing something, desperately anxious to avoid his searching eyes. She was trembling, shocked, shaken to discover in herself a vague disappointment at his sudden release of her. Resolutely she refused to recognise the stirrings of response to his kisses, the strength of his arms, the urgency of his passion. Firmly she told herself that she would not want the intimacy of his embrace even if he was gentle, tender, persuasive ... it was much less likely that he could arouse her with such cave-man tactics!

'I'm astonished that you are supposed to be so successful with women,' she said tautly. 'How did you earn your reputation as a marvellous lover, Max? Perhaps your kind of woman revels in rough handling. I don't! I won't be forced, Max! Once is too often!' All the bitterness in her swelling heart was behind the words.

His heart was stilled with shock. He was appalled by her version of his lovemaking. Certainly he had been urgent, impatient, rather too ardent and he knew that he had rushed her initiation into the sexual side of marriage and it would always be a matter of regret to him—but there had been no question of force! He was angered by the mere suggestion of it.

57

'I'm sorry it seemed like that to you,' he said quietly, trying to understand. 'Things must be very bad between us, Abigail. I wonder why you married me. I wonder even more if you already regret it!'

'Yes ... I do!' she returned impulsively, her chin lifting.

Max had known it but he had not expected her to admit it. Knowing the truth did not make it easier to accept when it was thrown at him so defiantly, so entirely without regard for his feelings. His eyes narrowed and hardened. 'I see,' he said grimly, very coldly.

There was something in his dark eyes that she had never seen before and she quailed slightly, knowing that she had gone too far. Max was not a man to take anything she cared to hand out without some form of retaliation ... and suddenly she knew that she did not wish to alienate him entirely beyond forgiveness. 'Oh, I'm sorry!' she said swiftly, awkwardly. 'I don't mean that, of course ... not exactly. It's just—oh, everything seems to be going wrong! Honeymoons are horrible!'

She sounded so youthfully disappointed, so genuinely remorseful, that it was impossible not to relent. 'This one is certainly a disaster,' he agreed wryly. His eyes softened as he looked down at her and knew again how much he loved her. 'Shall I take you home, Abigail?' he asked gently, thinking only of pleasing her, wondering if things might be better between

58

them if they left this place with all its unhappy associations. He doubted that they would return to this particular part of the French coast. The villa would always remind him of the hurt and the frustrations of this week ... and it suddenly occurred to him that Abigail's strange coldness towards him might depend to some extent on her awareness of the fact that he had entertained other women in these lovely surroundings. He was not sensitive to echoes from the past but Abigail might be, he decided.

'Oh please!' she exclaimed eagerly, too eagerly, her thoughts instantly winging to Toby who must still be in England and probably as anxious to see her as she was to see him. He had been constantly in her mind and heart and she knew that Max had suffered because of the resentment and frustration that was entirely due to her folly into rushing into this marriage when she had only ever wanted Toby. She was sorry for Max, of course ... but she was much sorrier for herself! There could be nothing worse in all the world than loving and wanting one man while knowing oneself tied to another!

Max nodded. 'Very well,' he said lightly. 'I'll go and make all the necessary arrangements right now. I see no reason why we shouldn't be home by this evening if it will please you.'

He was rewarded with a swift, spontaneous smile that struck him as being the warmest he had seen in her eyes all that week and it crossed his mind to wonder at her eagerness to return to England...

Abigail was dismayed to discover that 'home' meant Coneycroft, the big house on his Berkshire estate. She had foolishly assumed that they were bound for his flat in town and during the flight she had happily evolved a number of plans for getting in touch with Toby as soon as possible.

They crossed the channel in a privately chartered plane and a chauffeur-driven car was waiting for them at the airport. Max Constantine did not have wealth and influence for nothing! It was some little time before Abigail realised that they were not heading for London.

'Where are we, Max?' she asked curiously, leaning forward to scan the unfamiliar road.

'About ten miles from Coneycroft,' he said as though there was no question of going anywhere else. There was not as far as he was concerned. He refused to believe that his wife could love another man but he did think that Abigail had a weakness for her cousin Toby and he was determined to put as many miles as possible between her and temptation. He almost wished that Coneycroft was situated in the Hebrides!

'I thought we would spend a few days in town,' she said, not even trying to keep the dismay from her tone, too concerned to be discreet. 'I mean ... there are some things I want to do, Max—and we aren't expected at Coneycroft for another week! Must we go there?'

'Yes, I think we must,' he said pleasantly but with finality. 'I've already warned the staff of our return and I daresay everything is ready for us. I'm rather looking forward to a few days at Coneycroft before I must get back to work ... it's rather lovely at this time of year, you know.' He smiled at her. 'There's an important board meeting next week that I mustn't miss. I'll take you up to town with me then,' he assured her lightly.

Abigail was forced to resign herself to the situation but she was not at all pleased for it seemed only too likely that Toby would go back to Hollywood before they could meet and her heart sank at the very thought. For how could she see him if he was in London and she was buried in the heart of Berkshire with a husband who would probably keep her by his side as much as possible. It was all very well for Kate to tell her that Max would allow her to lead her own life without interference. She had a very strong suspicion that Max would do nothing of the sort!

Much too soon, the car swept up the long drive and came to a halt outside the main door of Coneycroft ... and Abigail looked up at the big old house in despair. It was not that she disliked Coneycroft. She had been impressed and thrilled when she first saw it—if a little

61

overawed by its grandeur and the realisation that she would be the new mistress. But in her overwrought state of mind the beautiful mansion seemed to represent a prison for she had married its master and given up all her freedom to do as she wished, go where she pleased and spend her time with whomever she liked ... unless Max approved!

A little later, she looked about the big and beautifully-furnished room that she was expected to share with Max and felt very near to tears. He had been born in this room and it was obviously expected that in due course his son would first see the light of day within its walls ... and she was supposed to provide him with that son! She felt trapped. She would not be able to shut Max out of this room so easily, she thought unhappily. Now that the honeymoon was over she doubted that he would be so tolerant, so patient, so undemanding.

She sat down on the edge of the wide bed— and leaped up as Max came into the room. She moved hastily away from the bed with all its implications, colour stealing into her face.

She was so obviously wary and apprehensive that Max knew that nothing had changed. It had been foolish to suppose that she might miraculously warm to him as soon as she crossed the threshold of her new home. For she was still set on keeping him at arms' length, he realised—and knew that he must continue to be patient if he wanted to win her in the end. It was essential that she should trust him, respond to him, welcome him into her arms... and until that day dawned he would make no demands upon her at all.

He smiled at her warmly. 'Welcome home, Abigail,' he said quietly and the warm tenderness in his voice when it touched on her name turned it into an endearment. He reached for her hands and stood looking down at her with a little glowing smile in his dark eyes.

'Yes ... thank you.' She swallowed and mustered a smile and went on as lightly as she could for the sudden pounding of her heart: 'It's rather baronial, isn't it? I'm a little overwhelmed. I don't think I'd quite realised...'

'What you were taking on?' he finished for her, a little drily. 'I'm sure you didn't.' He dropped her hands and turned away, knowing that she had been utterly deaf to his loving concern that she should be happy in her new home, utterly blind to the love and longing in his eyes. 'I do realise that everything will be a little strange at first and it will take time for you to get used to running this big house. But everyone is on your side and you may be sure of plenty of help and plenty of good advice from Mrs Powell.'

She wrinkled her shapely nose at the mention of the rather formidable housekeeper who had been at Coneycroft since long before

63

Max was born. 'I'm sure that Mrs Powell disapproves of me,' she said ruefully.

'Nonsense! All the staff are delighted with my choice of a bride. The daughter of General Sir Robert Carr ... what could be more suitable!' he demanded, smiling.

'Suitable...' she echoed, a little wryly. 'I suppose so. A marriage to mutual advantage ... or so my uncle described it.'

'I hope he may be right,' he said quietly and then went on briskly: 'We dine in ten minutes. There's no need to dress as we shall be alone. I'll go down and pour you a glass of sherry, shall I?'

CHAPTER SIX

Abigail sat up in the big bed, apprehensive eyes fixed on the door, ears straining for advance warning of Max's step in the corridor, her heart jumping at the slightest sound. She had expected him with every moment that had passed since she had left him enjoying a last drink and listening to the late news.

All evening, she had been tense with apprehension. Now she waited for him without the slightest anticipation of delight in his embrace.

She did not doubt that he would come to her. He had been very attentive, setting out to

64

please and entertain her, proving himself to be an ideal companion if only she had been in the mood to appreciate his efforts. But she had been much too aware that his attentions were only leading to the demands that she dreaded and knew she must no longer deny.

It seemed an eternity before she heard the sound that really did herald his approach. He came down the corridor, whistling softly, and Abigail fancied that he provided her with due warning of his invasion of the room. She tensed, waiting for the door to open ... but started nevertheless as Max appeared on the threshold of the room.

He paused, his heart contracting with love and longing for the slender girl against the pillows, pale hair tumbling gently about her shoulders, wide eyes regarding him in obvious apprehension. He smiled reassuringly and approached the big bed.

'Everything to your liking?' he asked lightly, smiling, speaking as easily as though she were a guest beneath his roof. 'Nothing that you need?'

'No, I don't think so,' she said, a little breathlessly.

'Right! Then I'll leave you to catch up on your beauty sleep.' He bent to brush his lips so lightly across her brow that it was not really a kiss at all. 'Pleasant dreams!'

He crossed the room to the door that led to the dressing-room beyond ... and a moment later Abigail was staring blankly at the wooden panels, utterly taken aback by the careless indifference of his manner.

She switched off the light and relaxed against the pillows, relieved—but at the same time she was puzzled, a little disconcerted, even annoyed that he should turn away when she had prepared herself to accept his lovemaking. In the dark, she lay with eyes wide open, studying the thin streak of light that showed beneath the communicating door, wondering if it was indifference or only pride that kept him from her arms. She knew that he had been angry, dismayed, perhaps even hurt and she appreciated that pride might be preventing him from making even the smallest gesture that might be interpreted as a sexual advance. But she had made up her mind not to rebuff him again. She knew that she had badly damaged the delicate fabric of their relationship. She realised that she had been unkind and unjust and unfeeling and it was not Max's fault that it all stemmed from her love for another man. She had known in good time that she did not want to marry Max after all and she should have found the courage and the resolution to say so. Having married him, she must make the best of it, she had decided—and having steeled herself to open her arms to him, it was infuriating to be left to sleep alone in this enormous bed in a big and rather lonely room. Max obviously did not want her at all, she thought crossly, quite forgetting that there had been no hint of a welcome in her own attitude—and she turned over, pushing him from her mind and concentrating on thoughts of Toby who would certainly never turn away from her so coldly if he was her husband!

Max read page after page of his book without absorbing a single word. But he knew it was useless to try to sleep just yet. Images of Abigail kept teasing and tormenting him and it took all his strength of mind to resist the temptation of all that loveliness in the adjoining room.

It had been a pleasant evening. It had seemed to him that she was a little more relaxed, a little more at ease, even a little encouraging ... and all his senses had been heightened by awareness of the warm and loving generosity that only needed the right touch to be released. He had felt that she was in a softer, more responsive mood and his heart had lifted with new hope and his blood had quickened with renewed desire ... until he went to join her and sensed the fear and revulsion rising as he approached.

Any man would have reacted exactly as he had, he thought wryly. No man with an ounce of sensitivity could want a woman who regarded him with obvious dislike and dread and shrank away from his slightest touch. All desire had died in a moment and he had found it astonishingly easy to wish her a careless goodnight and walk into his dressing-room.

The sexual disappointment did not really matter very much. What really hurt was the persistent rejection of his affection, his tender concern, his aching desire to love her and look after her and surround her with every happiness. He loved her deeply and he wanted her close to him on any terms and he knew that his patience could never run out. But it promised a very bleak future for them both unless she could be persuaded that he was not some kind of monster! She could not even bring herself to kiss him, it seemed. She had not made the smallest gesture of affection, the slightest overture, and it seemed very much out of character when he recalled the spontaneous warmth and sweetness of her earlier attitude. He could not rid himself of the growing suspicion that Cousin Toby was entirely to blame for the change of heart and the coldness and aversion that had ruined their honeymoon.

He looked up from his book in surprise as the communicating door opened abruptly. Abigail hesitated, a slight and appealing figure in a filmy nightgown of cream lace. 'Can I come in for a moment?' she asked in a small voice.

He put down his book. 'Of course,' he said lightly ... and only the slightest tremor in his voice betrayed that hope and desire surged together because she had come to him.

Abigail scarcely knew what had prompted the impulse. But she could not sleep and she had never felt so lonely or so miserable in her life. Dwelling on thoughts of Toby had been a mistake for it only emphasised the hopelessness of loving him now that she was married to Max. It was not an irrevocable step, of course. There was always divorce. But Abigail had a great deal of pride and she shrank from a public admission that her marriage was a mistake ... particularly as everyone would assume that Max, a confirmed bachelor for years, was the one who regretted relinquishing his freedom, she thought bitterly. She did not think she could bear the comment and the gossip and the speculation that would sweep through their circle of friends if their marriage was to end before it had properly begun!

'I don't seem to be able to sleep,' she said, a little lamely. 'There's an owl...'

It hooted even as she spoke. Max smiled tenderly. 'City girl,' he teased. 'You can sleep with all the noise of London's traffic in your ears but a solitary owl can keep you awake down here!'

'Silly, isn't it?' she agreed, striving for lightness. She was suddenly, desperately shy before that smile in his dark eyes. He was so nice and she had treated him very badly and still he could forgive and behave with warmth towards her, she thought on a sudden wave of affection for him. It was silly to regard him as an enemy and tell herself that he cared nothing for her ... he must be fond of her or he would not have married her! He was not really the kind of man to marry only for the sake of getting an heir—and even if he was he might have chosen a wife from among a dozen women. If he had wished to marry her then he must have had good reason. 'I expect I shall get used to it,' she went on, smiling. 'I'm disturbing you, Max ... I'm sorry! I'll go away!'

She looked ridiculously young and utterly enchanting with her bare toes just peeping beneath the hem of the long lacy nightgown and her small and very lovely face framed by the soft, tumbling hair. His heart went out to her with such a rush of loving tenderness that it actually hurt!

He held out his hand. 'Don't run away, Abby,' he said softly, love and longing in his tone and tenderness touching the depths of his dark eyes.

Abigail was startled. She had never heard that particular note in his voice before ... and it was unfortunate that he should sound so much like Toby! It was the first time that she had realised a certain similarity in their voices. She wished he had not shortened her name just as Toby did and with just that kind of melting warmth that always tugged at her heart... for he was not Toby and never could be Toby and she ached with love for Toby and would not

70

settle for second-best!

She drew back abruptly ... aware that she had been incredibly near to melting into his arms and forgetting everything but her need of love and tenderness and affection. She was shocked to find a degree of yearning within her to be close to him, to lie in his arms ... and she knew it could only be born of her loneliness and her aching need for the man she really loved and wanted.

There was panic in her beautiful eyes—and Max could not know that she was alarmed by the force of her own emotions rather than any desire she sensed in him. He was flooded with disappointment and suddenly angry. 'What a child you are, Abigail,' he said wearily.

She mistook regret for contempt. Her chin tilted. 'I daresay you think so!' she said angrily. 'You're so used to mature women, aren't you ... women of the world!' Her tone was scathing. 'I can't think why you wanted to marry me!'

Impatience touched his eyes. 'Don't be foolish,' he said curtly.

She bridled. 'It isn't so foolish. We aren't really suited to each other at all!' There was angry defiance in her tone.

He raised an eyebrow. 'No? I thought we were remarkably well suited—and I understood that you thought so, too.'

'Yes ... but then I didn't know—I didn't realise...' She broke off, disconcerted. She had

71

come dangerously close to blurting out her dismay when she had looked into Toby's blue eyes and known that she loved him ... on the very day that she had married Max!

'You knew what marriage entailed, surely,' he said quietly, pulling gently at the lobe of his ear.

Abigail looked blank—and then realised that he had misunderstood her discomfiture. 'Oh, I'm not talking about sex!' she declared impatiently. 'There's much more to marriage than that!'

A wry smile tugged at his lips. 'Very true,' he agreed drily. 'But you've a lot to learn if you suppose that it can be dismissed so lightly!'

She fancied there was reproach behind the words. It might be justified but she instinctively resented it. 'I don't dismiss the importance of an heir to a man in your position,' she said carefully. 'It's why you married me, of course ... and I'm prepared to have a child, Max. But you must give me time—and you might try persuading me that sex can be wonderful instead of making me feel that it's only a means to an end!'

A nerve jumped in his lean cheek. He marvelled that she could be so blind, so insensitive to the love that had swept him inexorably towards marriage. Anger surged that she could ignore every expression of his love and suppose that his need to share his life

72

with her and his desire for their mutual delight in each other only sprang from a cold-blooded wish for a son!

'Suddenly I seem to have lost all interest in becoming a father,' he drawled, cold with anger. 'So it's just as well that I already have an heir ... my nephew, Jessica's boy! You needn't worry your pretty head about obliging me, Abigail. Frankly, I don't think you are mature enough for marriage let alone motherhood!'

The quiet words were all the more forceful because she knew that they were well deserved—but she wondered how she had offended when she had only brought truth out into the open! It seemed so silly to go on pretending that theirs was anything other than a marriage of convenience!

There was iron in his tone and the look in his eyes sent a tiny shiver along her spine. It was very important that they should be friends, she abruptly realised ... she was alarmed to discover that he was regarding her with something very like cold contempt. 'Don't look that way, Max,' she said impetuously. 'I didn't mean to make you angry—and surely we can talk about these things without losing our tempers?'

Max sighed. 'Oh, go back to bed, Abigail,' he said roughly. 'You are only making matters worse!'

She stiffened and her eyes sparked with indignation. She turned away with quiet

73

dignity and left him ... and shed a few angry tears in the privacy of the big bed that she should never have left in a foolish attempt to reach a better understanding with the man she had married!

They met at breakfast. Fully prepared to find him nursing a sense of grievance and determined to behave as though nothing had happened for her part, Abigail was astonished when he greeted her pleasantly and produced a number of suggestions for their entertainment during the day. Relieved, even thankful that there was no open breach between them, she was very ready to follow his lead.

They spent a week at Coneycroft before informing any of their family or friends that they had cut short their honeymoon in the South of France. They tramped through woods and over fields with the dogs. They rode over miles of beautiful countryside. They fished in the little stream that ran through the estate. They went for long drives in search of quaint pubs and ancient churches and secluded picnic spots. They played tennis. They swam in the lake and lazed in the sun and assured each other that no one needed the South of France while the whole of England basked in a heat-wave. They listened to music and played backgammon and read books and watched some television and idly discussed a thousand and one subjects without ever touching on the personal.

It would have been an idyllic week for a newly-wed couple in love with each other. Abigail found it a strain and doubted that Max could be so content as he seemed with the strangeness of the situation. She felt very much a guest in her new home. Max was the perfect host—and she might be the wife of his best friend! He was courteous, attentive, considerate—and quite impersonal, she felt. They were together for much of each day but she did not know if he wanted it that way or if he would have preferred to occupy his time with other matters and other company.

It was a relief to accompany him to town and she relaxed a little at the thought of spending some time with friends and family. Looking back, it seemed to Abigail that Max had not shown her any tenderness or affection or real warmth such as a wife had a right to expect from her husband and she was resentful ... quite forgetting that she had been keeping him at arm's length ever since their wedding night!

She was more than resentful, she suddenly discovered. She was inexplicably furious! For Max just did not care! He did not give a snap of his fingers for the state of their marriage or for the tensions that were building up in her. It was all very well for Max! Marriage was only a means to an end for him although he professed to be indifferent to the need for an heir ... and for his sexual satisfaction there would always be other women, no doubt! But Abigail had

75

nothing to comfort her when she contemplated a bleak future with the man who cared so little for her. She did not want or expect Max to love her ... he was obviously incapable of any real feeling for her. But she had hoped that affection and understanding might create a foundation for a lasting and reasonably successful marriage, she thought bitterly.

Utterly without experience and with no one to advise her, Abigail was at a loss. She did not know what to do for the best. She did not want Max to make love to her with alarming passion but she certainly did not want him to be so cold and distant towards her. It was not very pleasant to live with his impersonal attitude, his careless indifference, his utter insensitivity to her need for affection and approval.

Abigail wandered about the sitting-room of the luxurious penthouse flat that overlooked Hyde Park. Max was in his study attending to various business matters that had accumulated during his absence from town. Very sure that he had already dismissed her from his mind, she felt a little lonely and despairing—and on a sudden impulse she reached for the telephone. There was one man who would not fail her, she thought defiantly—and she had wasted too much time already on resisting temptation ...

CHAPTER SEVEN

It was a wet and dismal morning. It seemed that their arrival in town had coincided with the end of the heat-wave, Abigail thought with regret. She looked at the heavy clouds and incessant rain and felt despondent ... and yet she had every reason to be happy and excited on this particular day. For she was only hours away from being with Toby!

She had managed to reach him at his London club and her heart had been warmed by his eager delight at the sound of her voice on the telephone. Knowing that Max had an important meeting and would be too busy to know or care how she spent her day, she had arranged to meet Toby for lunch and her whole being had been focused on the moment of their meeting ever since she woke.

She knew she should mention her plans to Max with the casual, light-hearted assumption that he would approve. Toby was cousin as well as close friend and he might not be long in England and it was very natural that she should wish to see something of him. But it was not at all easy to mention Toby to Max, she found, glancing at his rather grave face as he studied the Financial Times. He could not know how she felt about Toby, of course. He had no reason to be suspicious and it was unlikely that he would be jealous. Yet each time she resolved to refer lightly to her lunch engagement, the words seemed to shrivel on her tongue.

She really did not want to meet Toby without telling Max. But it seemed very difficult, even impossible, to tell him! Supposing he disliked the idea, expressed disapproval, even tried to forbid her! One never knew with Max, she thought wryly, very much aware that she had married a stranger. She must see Toby! Nothing else seemed to matter. She was impatient, restless, desperate to be with him if only for a brief hour. She dreaded the thought that he might soon go back to America and it could be months or even years before they met again!

She would not wish to defy Max, she admitted, and deceit could be foolish, even dangerous. But it did not seem the wisest thing in the world to mention Toby just now. Things were not too good between her and Max ... and there was really no need to make a mountain out of a molehill, she told herself brightly. There was absolutely no reason why she should not lunch with her cousin ... and Max would probably be pleased to know that she was being well looked after while he attended to the board meeting and other business of the Constantine Construction Company.

The honeymoon was over and Abigail had a

78

feeling that she would be relegated to a relatively unimportant place in his life for he thrived on the demands and responsibilities of the company that his grandfather had founded. There were many other concerns in which he had an interest, too ... far too many for her to know much about them. She was not really interested ... and Max had never been in the habit of discussing business matters with her.

She hoped that they would live for the most part in this comfortable penthouse flat with its superb panoramic view of London. For she had plenty of friends and plenty to occupy her in town whereas she would soon grow bored at Coneycroft for all its beauty and splendour.

She reached for the marmalade and Max put down his newspaper, reminded of her presence by the movement. He smiled at her pleasantly. 'What do you mean to do today?' he asked lightly. 'Would you like to have lunch with me?'

Her heart plunged. He could not possibly know of her telephone call to Toby and her desperate determination to meet him come what may. It could only be guilt that made her feel so uncomfortable and search so desperately for an acceptable excuse.

'Oh, Max, I've so much I want to do,' she said, a little too quickly. 'People to see, a hair appointment ... and I have some shopping to do, too. I really couldn't guarantee to be in a

79

certain place at a certain time!'

He nodded, wondering if he would ever become inured to the pain and disappointment she could inflict so easily, so thoughtlessly. She was making it much too obvious that she would prefer to do anything rather than meet him for lunch. He supposed it was natural that she should want a breathing-space. They had virtually lived in each other's pockets for over a fortnight and he only wished it could have been a more satisfactory time for them both.

'Very well,' he said lightly. 'It was just a passing thought. You will have some lunch, though, Abigail? Don't be too busy to bother!'

'Oh, I'll snatch a sandwich between shopping and having my hair done,' she said lightly but a little colour stole into her face. She turned the subject. 'What are your plans, Max? Do you mean to stay in town? There's a new play at the Ibex and James Donoghue has an exhibition in Bond Street next week—and there's Cecily's birthday party at the weekend!' It was important that she should know what was happening before she saw Toby, she thought, hoping that she might have several opportunities of seeing him before Max whisked her back to Coneycroft.

Max hesitated. He had meant to stay only overnight in town. He felt that he and Abigail had more chance of settling their differences in the quiet, peaceful and undemanding surroundings of his country home. He sensed that she would soon fill her life with social engagements and push him further away each day that passed if they stayed in town. But he knew that it would be fatal to all his hopes if he held her on too tight a rein. He had never been possessive or demanding—but then he had never loved anyone until now, he thought wryly.

'Whatever you wish,' he said, smiling. 'You don't have to answer to me, you know—or seek my approval for anything you wish to do. You have your own circle of friends, of course. There are things that interest and amuse you that I really won't have time to share with you, I'm afraid. I won't be able to give as much time to you as I should like so I can scarcely object if you make your own social arrangements for much of the time.'

Abigail felt uneasy. He was giving her *carte blanche* to do exactly as she pleased—and she ought to be delighted. But she could not help feeling that it was unnatural that he should be so casual, so disinterested. Surely he knew that he was opening the door to all manner of disloyalties—and she only wished that she was strong enough to resist the temptation that was Toby!

Max watched the swift play of expression cross her lovely face and felt that he had a very good idea of the thoughts that went through her mind. He was saddened but there was very little he could do. Whether or not he gave his approval, she would go where she wished and see whom she pleased, he thought wryly. She was very young and a little wilful and she did not care enough to consider his feelings. She did not even realise that they existed—and he wondered if it was a case of not wanting to know! Perhaps she preferred to ease her conscience with the belief that he had only married for an heir and chosen her because she was 'suitable'. The more he revolved events in his mind the more convinced he became that Abigail had taken him for material and social gain and had never felt the smallest degree of real affection for him. He had supposed that he was whisking her to the altar before she could change her mind but in truth she had been anxious to marry him before he realised that her warmth and sweetness was all pretence!

He pushed back his chair and rose from the table. 'Enjoy yourself, my dear,' he said, briefly resting his hand on her shoulder and knowing that she tensed at his touch. He smiled down at her. 'Would you like me to organise seats at the Ibex for this evening ... it's the first night, isn't it.'

'I'd like that,' she agreed, returning his smile—and wishing he would not try to please her! It only made her feel ridiculously guilty about meeting Toby... and she ought not to feel guilty about spending a little time with her own cousin, after all! 'I hope your meeting goes well, Max,' she added with belated interest...

Toby was waiting for her with a hint of a lover's impatience in the way he scanned the entrance for her arrival. Seeing him, Abigail felt a surge of tenderness, thinking that he had never possessed the gift of patience. He had always wanted what he wanted when he wanted it! And such was his charm and his confidence that life had never let him down ... until the woman he loved had married another man. Abigail's heart abruptly filled with regret for the disappointment she had inflicted on him as well as herself—and she hurried to him with love and longing in her expressive eyes.

Toby rose at her approach. He looked down at her for a tense moment. Then he placed his hands on her shoulders and bent to kiss her, quite regardless of the fact that they met in a public place and that one or both of them might easily be recognised by the gossips who frequented the famous restaurant. 'Abby...' he said warmly, admiringly, smiling into her eyes.

She was too full for words. She could only smile at him ... a soft, tremulous smile that illuminated her small face.

They waited for the drinks he had ordered. She sat beside him, her hand clasped firmly in his possessive grasp as though he meant never to let her go again. Excitement caused her heart to throb almost painfully. She was so happy to be with him and so thankful that he loved her still and so ready to forget everything but the delight in this brief hour with him.

The drinks came and he raised his glass to her, a compelling intensity in his blue eyes. 'You are so lovely,' he said, a little roughly. 'Constantine doesn't deserve you, Abby!'

Instinctively she recoiled. Swiftly she touched her fingers to his lips. 'Please ... don't spoil things,' she said softly. 'I don't want to think about Max just now. I just want to enjoy being with you.'

He was silent, studying her with thoughtful eyes. Then he said: 'You look very well. Marriage agrees with you, I guess.'

She met his eyes steadily. 'Looks can be deceptive, Toby.'

He raised an eyebrow. 'Don't you like being married, Abby?' he drawled, a little mockingly.

She shrugged. 'I imagine that it would be wonderful—with the right man,' she said deliberately. She did not mean to pretend with Toby. It was impossible to deceive him, anyway. He was much too perceptive to suppose that she loved Max or had found any happiness in her impulsive marriage.

'Constantine seemed to be the right man when I last saw you,' he said smoothly. 'You were a very radiant bride—and you are positively glowing right now! You're such a splendid advertisement for the married state that I'm tempted to try it for myself!'

Abigail winced. He was so hurt that he wanted to hurt her, she knew ... and forgave

84

him instantly. 'The glow is for you, Toby,' she said gently. She reached for his hand and smiled at him with her heart in her eyes. 'Oh, Toby, it's wonderful to see you!'

He ran his thumb lightly across the smooth skin of her wrist in a careless caress. 'It's wonderful to see you, my sweet,' he said. 'I'm very fond of you.'

'Yes, I know,' she said achingly, knowing that the words could only be an understatement of his real feelings. He loved her just as she loved him—but it was a hopeless situation! 'Toby, I'm so sorry!' she blurted suddenly, the words wrung from her heart.

He was absently turning the wedding band on her finger. 'Sorry ...?' he echoed.

'I don't really know how it happened,' she said helplessly. 'I hardly know Max and I certainly don't love him. I didn't mean to marry him. I didn't plan to marry anyone but you, Toby. But I haven't seen you for so long and it's months since you wrote and I knew you were dating other women—oh, I think I missed you so much and Max was so nice and seemed so fond of me ... I don't know how it happened,' she said again, finding it almost impossible to explain even to herself why she had been so sure that marrying Max was right and natural and all she could want—until the moment of marrying him arrived! 'I think Max must have hypnotised me or something,' she added ruefully. 'It was all so unreal... just like

85

a dream!'

'Very romantic,' he said drily. 'Swept off your feet by the handsome stranger! I suppose you knew nothing of his millions until you left the church with his ring on your finger? Oh, come on, Abby! Everyone knows just why you married him and I don't know that I blame you! It must be very pleasant to be Lady Constantine—and there isn't much security in being the wife of a struggling actor even if I'd ever asked you to marry me!'

'Well ... we always knew that we loved each other,' Abigail said, a little defensively, suddenly discovering that she did not know this new Toby at all. The cynicism and the sarcasm were disturbing.

'Oh, I love you,' he said as carelessly as though he spoke of the weather. 'There's no one quite like you, after all. But that doesn't mean that I can't live without you—and I daresay you'll find that you can live quite happily with Constantine. He's good to you, isn't he ... treats you right?'

'It doesn't really matter, does it,' she said bleakly. 'I married him and I shall have to stay with him. There doesn't seem to be any alternative.' Her heart was sick and heavy with disappointment. She did not know what she had expected Toby to say or do but she supposed she had imagined he would rescue her as he had so many times before, extricating her from scrapes with admirable ease and promptitude.

'Oh, there's an alternative,' he said easily. 'Come and live with me, Abby. I shall shortly be going back to Hollywood and I'll take you with me. I'll look after you, darling.' He watched her small, flower-like face for reaction and saw the dark-blue eyes widen with anxiety.

'Oh, Toby—I wish I could!' she exclaimed unhappily. It was only a dream, of course... the kind of fantasy she had been weaving ever since her wedding day! But it bore no resemblance at all to reality. A bride of little more than a fortnight could not leave her husband for another man. She really had no right to be thinking of Toby with love and it was very wrong to be meeting him like this, she thought with a twinge of guilt.

Toby regarded her with a little smile in his eyes, feeling that he knew her very much better than she knew herself. She was a romantic child—but there was a very strong streak of common-sense in her make-up and she would not wreck a very good marriage for his sake.

'Do you?' he said quizzically.

'Oh yes!' she declared, sighing. 'It would be wonderful to be with you for always, Toby.'

'Then it's settled? You'll come to me?'

'How can I? It just isn't possible,' she said unhappily. She swirled the wine in her glass. 'Are you really going back to America?'

'Of course I am! I've a great future in films over there... and there's nothing to keep me in

87

England,' he said firmly.

'Not even me,' she murmured.

'My sweet, you're a married woman,' he pointed out drily. 'Obviously you don't wish to change anything or you wouldn't be hesitating. I guess you really care more for Constantine than you think, Abby. You've grown out of your love for me, after all.'

'No!' she protested swiftly, very sure. 'I do love you! Max just happened!' She stretched her hand to him. 'I don't feel anything for him, truly!'

'Well, you don't have to stay with him,' he said carelessly. 'It's your choice, Abby ... me or his millions. You've only a few weeks in which to decide what you really want.'

Abigail was touched that he really wanted her—much more than his casual attitude implied. It might seem that he did not care whether she went with him to America or stayed with Max but she was confident that it would be a bitter blow to him if she chose Max. She only wished it was a matter of choice! She simply did not feel that she could walk out on her marriage before she had given it a fair chance!

Toby changed the subject, dismissing the problem of her future for the time being, and he talked at length of Hollywood and the studios and the famous and the way of life that was vastly different to anything he had known in England. Abigail listened with interest ...

88

and found herself wondering if it could ever be her way of life.

She loved Toby dearly but she was not blind to his innate selfishness and she realised that she would have to do most of the giving if she lived with him. It was not an easy decision to make, she thought wryly. Toby could go away for a year and scarcely think of her, seldom write to her ... and it would not cross his mind that she would not be waiting for him when he returned. In fact, that was exactly what had happened, Abigail thought ruefully—and for the first time she wondered if it had been the contrast between Toby's casual and careless acceptance and Max's warm and eager persuasions that had swayed her emotions and swept her into marriage...

CHAPTER EIGHT

Max crossed the rain-soaked pavement to reach his waiting car ... and paused when he was hailed by a familiar and friendly voice. He turned, his swift smile instantly warming his handsome face as Kate ran towards him in a bright yellow raincoat and matching hat. He was very fond of Kate. They were very good friends and the fact that they had never been lovers belied the usual implication of the description.

89

She gave him her hands in obvious delight, no longer concerned with the rain and the hundred and one other irritations that had besieged her day. 'Max!' she said warmly. 'How nice!'

He kissed her cheek, responding instinctively to the affection and admiration that seemed such a welcome contrast to Abigail's current attitude to him. 'Where are you going? Will you lunch with me?' he suggested swiftly, almost eagerly.

'Of course I will!' she said gaily. 'Why do you think I ran so hard to catch you!'

Max laughed and opened the car door for her. She sat back on the comfortable seat with a little sigh of appreciation. Within moments, the white Rolls Royce glided gently into the stream of traffic. 'I thought the Caprice,' Max said lightly. 'Is it still your favourite place for lunch?'

She was pleased that he remembered—but that was one of the nice things about Max, she thought a little wistfully. 'Me and a thousand others!' she declared, smiling. 'We shall never get a table, Max!'

'Oh, I don't anticipate any difficulty,' he said with all the confidence of a man who knew himself instantly recognised and swiftly obliged by the staff in such places.

Kate pulled off her hat and ran her slender fingers through the silken cap of her hair. She smiled at him. 'This is nice,' she said

90

appreciatively, indicating the car's comfortable interior. 'I could get used to this kind of luxury, Max. I envy your wife a little!'

He laughed. 'How do you know she wouldn't happily change places with you by this time?' he said lightly but there was a slight edge to the words.

Kate chuckled at the utter absurdity of the suggestion. It was ludicrous to suppose that Max of all men could not make Abigail or any other woman happy! Deep down, she really did envy her cousin a little. She was far from being in love with Max but she was very fond of him and she trusted him more than any man she knew and she would have married him if he had offered the opportunity, confident that her second venture into matrimony would be much more successful than the first if only because they were friends where as she and Silas had never been anything more than lovers who should not have made the mistake of marrying.

'How is Abby?' she asked warmly. 'Is she in town?'

'She's very well,' he said smoothly, giving nothing away. 'She came up to town with me yesterday. I've been at a board meeting all morning so Abigail is taking the opportunity to do some shopping and meet some friends.'

'Then she won't mind if I monopolise you for an hour,' she said lightly. 'I'm so glad I ran into you, Max. I've had a foul morning and I desperately need a sympathetic ear!'

Max was equally glad of the chance encounter with the attractive, intelligent Kate. It was very pleasant to be with her, to bask in her affection and admiration, to feel more relaxed than he had for days. There could be no strain, no demands on his emotions, no sexual tension in his relationship with Kate, he decided thankfully ... and it was not disloyal to Abigail to enjoy her cousin's company. She was a very likeable and generous person and a good friend. Their affection for each other had survived for some years. He had known and admired Kate long before her disastrous marriage and he had supported her through the messy and painful divorce. He had been of financial help from time to time in those days and he was now a sleeping partner in her successful venture as a fashion designer. And he had Kate to thank for that introduction to the girl he had loved on sight!

Now he wondered if she had played some part in persuading Abigail to marry him for she was devoted to his interests, he knew. She was fond of him and therefore concerned for his happiness—and he did not doubt that she understood just how much he loved and needed her youthful cousin. She might even have been fully aware that Abigail did not care for him but dismissed any qualms with the ease of someone who knew and liked him well and felt sure that he could persuade any woman to love him. He thought wryly that he had been equally confident.

He spent a pleasant hour with Kate at the Caprice. The seating arrangements and the soft, intimate lighting and the fact that his attention was centred on his companion made it possible for him to be separated from his wife by only a few yards and yet be completely unaware of her presence...

Abigail gave herself up to the magic of the moment, thrusting to the back of her mind Toby's suggestion that she should go away with him. She needed time to consider. She was aware that he made light love to her with his smiling eyes, his teasing voice, the casual caress in the touch of his hand and her heart responded eagerly to his nearness. But she hesitated to give him the answer that he obviously desired.

She had been too impulsive in agreeing to marry Max. So she must be very sure that it was right for them both before she agreed to trust her future to Toby's care. It would be a very difficult step for her to take, she thought ruefully, knowing the horror and the scandal that her behaviour would provoke. No one would have a good word to say for a runaway bride! Her family would be shocked and appalled. Her friends would never understand how she could do such a thing. Most important of all, she had to live with herself ... and she was not sure that she could steel herself to

93

behave quite so badly!

So she refused to think about it for the time being ... and she talked, laughed, reminisced with Toby with a seemingly light heart...

When they rose to wend their way through the tables, Max saw his wife and her companion. The man's arm was about her slender waist and his head was bent to murmur something in her ear, his eyes warm with admiration and obvious intent—and Abigail, utterly careless of appearances, smiled up at him and touched her hand to his cheek in an unmistakable gesture of love.

Max might have managed to convince himself that it was an innocent rendezvous if he had not witnessed that particular scene. But they were so obviously lovers that his heart jolted with dismay—and then turned to ice. A nerve throbbed abruptly in his jaw and his eyes were like chips of granite as he watched them leave the restaurant. He was not angry. He was numb. He wanted very much to be angry, to hurry after them, to rant and rave and revel in knocking the man down with one killing blow. But he could not feel anything. It was just as though it was happening to someone else ... or as though he watched the scene on film. His wife walked through a restaurant with her lover for all the world to see. And there was nothing he could do about it!

He did not care. It did not matter. He was merely irritated that she had so little thought that she advertised her preference for another man so openly.

Kate broke off in the middle of a sentence, aware that he was not listening. She turned her head to discover what absorbed his attention but could see nothing to account for that particular grimness of his expression. She was unaware that her two cousins had just passed out of sight. 'What is it?' she asked, a little anxiously. For he looked ill, she suddenly realised. He was ashen and very tense like a man in pain. 'Max darling, what's the matter?'

He looked at her without seeing her for a moment. He had completely forgotten Kate. He had not seen her animated face or heard her eager voice or felt the light touch of her hand. All his world had been momentarily caught up in the shock of discovering that the woman he loved existed only in his mind! For where was the sweet sincerity and generous warmth and quiet simplicity of the Abigail who had swept him into loving? Where was the affectionate and trusting girl with all the enchanting sweetness and candour that he had thought so necessary to his happiness? The girl he had married was cold and unfeeling and selfish, scurrying to meet her lover at the first opportunity, foolish or careless enough to flaunt her disloyalty in a public place. She was a stranger and a cheat that he could not even like!

He pulled himself together, even managed a

smile. 'Sorry ... you were saying?'

'What is it, Max?' Kate demanded again, searching his handsome face. 'You looked awful. I thought you were about to throw a heart attack!' she added bluntly, relieved as some of his tension seemed to recede and some colour returned to his face.

He covered her hand with his own in a swift gesture of appreciation for her concern. Dear Kate! He had been a fool to fall headlong in love with her cousin's lovely face when there was someone like Kate who really deserved a second chance at happiness and might have found it with him! There might have been no highs or lows in marriage with Kate but he could have been content—and he would have known exactly where he stood! For Kate was straightforward in all her dealings. Kate was just the kind of wife that a man like him really needed. But he had fallen for her lovely cousin and set her on a pedestal and determined to marry her with all the eagerness and unsuspecting trust of an inexperienced boy! And he was paying the penalty for that mistake!

'Don't worry,' he said reassuringly. 'I'm all right now, Kate. It was nothing ... just a passing spasm.' Thus he lightly dismissed the weeks of loving and longing and was thankful that he was his own master once more. He was no longer at the mercy of the emotional see-saw called love...

Toby had plenty of time on his hands and wished to spend it with Abigail ... and she was very happy to please him. The rain had stopped and a watery sun was breaking through the clouds when they left the Caprice and so they walked hand in hand through the rain-soaked park until they reached the Serpentine where Toby insisted on hiring a boat and showing off his skill as an oarsman ... and Abigail admired and applauded him and delighted in their togetherness and resolutely refused to dwell on the thought that very soon they must separate and she must go back to the flat and Max.

They left the lake and strolled like lovers with arms about each other ... and Toby paused to kiss her, careless of amused and interested passers-by. It was a light and undemanding and wholly affectionate kiss and Abigail was grateful for its lack of passion. She had experienced the fierce urgency of a man's desire without pleasure or understanding and she was relieved that Toby's kiss was so gentle and sexless.

It grew late and they turned their steps towards the towering block of flats that overlooked the park with its penthouse apartment that Max owned.

Abigail had a little difficulty in persuading Toby that it was not wise or possible for her to dine and dance with him that evening. He did not seem to appreciate that she could no longer do just as she liked, she thought ruefully. Just

97

because she loved him and not her husband and admitted it without shame he seemed to think that she need not consider Max at all!

'So when do I see you?' he asked impatiently.

'Darling, I don't know,' she said helplessly. 'I'll try to make it soon ... you know I'll try! But it isn't easy for me. I mustn't make Max suspicious, after all.'

He looked down at her with a mocking little smile in his blue eyes. 'Does it really matter? Do you really care? You know very well that you've no intention of staying with him. You belong to me!' He lifted her hand to his lips and pressed a kiss into the palm, closing her fingers over it... and his eyes, gazing into her own, compelled her to agree, to prove the love she professed to have for him!

Still she hesitated. 'It's all so simple for you,' she said slowly, almost resentfully.

'I don't know why you are making a difficulty of it, Abby!' he exclaimed with a hint of impatience. 'Give me an answer! Yes or no? Either you love me or you don't!'

'I do! Of course I do!' she almost wailed, clutching his hand and gazing up at him with near desperation in her dark-blue eyes. 'But you make it seem so easy—and it isn't, Toby! How do I tell Max that I'm going to live with you instead of him—when I've only just married him!'

'Don't tell him,' he said curtly. 'Leave the traditional note! Good Lord, Abby, do you expect him to smile and give you his blessing? I don't want to deal with an irate husband—and we don't want the whole world involved as it will be if you go around telling people what you mean to do!' Suddenly he grinned. '*Fait accompli*, Abby—it's the only way!'

'Yes, I suppose so,' she said with a doubtful sigh. She did not smile. She would not admit it even to herself but she felt a little angry with him. She thought that all this upheaval might have been spared if only he had come back to England a little sooner—or even written to her when her engagement was announced. He had not lifted a finger to prevent her from marrying Max... but he expected her to run away with him now without a thought for anyone else or anything but their happiness. She need never have married Max if only he had spoken ... and she would not be wondering now if she could bear the turmoil that must result if she left Max after only a fortnight of marriage.

Toby was exultant, sure that he had won. He had always thought of Abigail as his property and he had assumed that she knew that he meant to marry her one day. He did not blame her for rushing into an impulsive marriage with Constantine ... the temptations and the pressures put upon her must have been very great. If she had known any affection for the man she had married, if she seemed at all likely to be happy with him, he would have gone back to America without making any claim to her and continued to enjoy life sufficiently well without her. But Abigail loved him and she had not been able to conceal it even on her wedding day—and he did not feel that he could let her down. The fact that she had turned to him at the earliest opportunity proved that her marriage was a mistake. Toby was very willing to take her away and look after her and he had no sympathy to spare for Constantine. If a man could not make his wife happy in the first weeks of marriage then he deserved to lose her!

'Then it's settled,' he said firmly. 'You're coming with me, Abby. There's nothing to keep us in this country so I'll arrange a couple of seats on the first flight to New York.'

Abigail suddenly saw the white Rolls Royce with its distinctive number plate approaching on the other side of the road.

She rushed into hasty speech. 'Yes, all right, Toby. I will come! But don't make any plans yet. Don't rush me! I must go, Toby ... Max is home! I'll ring you...'

He smiled down at her. 'So he'll see us together,' he said easily. 'So what? It isn't a crime to lunch with me, is it? I'll walk over with you and you can introduce me to Constantine ... how about it?'

She panicked at the mere suggestion. 'Oh no!' She jerked her hand from his arm. 'I know what I'm doing, Toby ... please don't make it any more difficult than it is!' She sent him a shaky and rather rueful smile and left him,

100

hoping that Max had not noticed them as he stepped from the car and made his way across the pavement to the main entrance of the flats.

The lift was on its way to the penthouse and she waited for it to return, thankful for the brief breathing-space before she faced Max. She was elated after hours with Toby and she was sure it must show. Her blood was tingling and her heart was beating a little too fast from mingled excitement and guilt. It was all very well for Toby to claim that it was not a crime for cousins to meet for lunch but she would have felt as guilty as any criminal if she had been seen with Toby at the Caprice. She comforted herself with the thought that Max had probably been much too busy to bother with lunch and that the Caprice was not one of his favourite haunts, anyway.

She thrust to the very back of her mind all thoughts of that hasty agreement with Toby. It had been inevitable, of course, in view of the disaster that her marriage to Max had turned out to be ... but she did not want to think just now about the actuality of leaving him or the consequences...

CHAPTER NINE

Max was busy at the decanters and merely glanced at her without interest as she entered.

She was flooded with relief . . . and she smiled at him with real warmth, thankful that she would not be called upon to explain the hours she had spent with Toby. 'Oh, Max!' she exclaimed as if she had not expected to see him. 'I meant to be back before you! But it's been such a day!'

He drank some whiskey, contemplating her with an enigmatic expression in his dark eyes. He had seen her on the other side of the road, deep in conversation with her cousin. The slender figure in the white trouser suit was much too distinctive to miss. They had obviously spent most of the day together and felt all the regret and reluctance of lovers at having to part. 'No parcels,' he said, a little dry.

Momentarily, Abigail looked blank. 'Oh . . . my shopping!' she exclaimed, comprehending. 'As it happened, I only window-shopped . . . didn't see anything I liked enough to buy!' she declared lightly. It ought to have been easy to lie to him—but there was such a disquieting expression in his eyes that she found herself faltering, colouring, speaking much too quickly.

'You didn't find time for your hair appointment,' he commented with apparent carelessness.

Abigail put a hand to the hair that tumbled untidily about her face and shoulders, tossed by wind and rain, tousled by Toby's affectionate hand. 'I . . . I made a mistake in the date,' she said hastily. 'So silly! My appointment is for tomorrow!'

Max regarded her with dislike. A cheat and a liar, he thought with contempt. He felt a faint surprise that he had wanted her so much that nothing else had mattered. It had obviously not been love at all but a madness in his blood, he thought wryly ... for nothing was left of all that emotion. 'Convenient,' he drawled with faint mockery.

Apprehension stirred. 'Oh ... are you going to be busy?' she asked uncertainly. 'Do you have plans for tomorrow?'

'I expect you have,' he said coldly, turning to the decanter and refilling his glass. 'Won't you be meeting Cousin Toby?'

Her heart lurched and she felt slightly sick.

'Oh ... did you see us?' she said lamely. 'I met him by chance... in the park.'

He looked at her for a long moment. 'I took Kate to lunch today, Abigail. We went to the Caprice. I don't think you were there by chance ... but say so if I'm mistaken.'

The colour stormed into her small face and she looked so guilty that his lip curled with contempt. She made a desperate attempt at recover.

'I wish I'd seen you, Max. Why didn't you come over to our table? I want you to know Toby and we might have joined forces.'

'There are times when two is obviously company and others are very much *de trop*,' he said.

103

'Oh yes ... but I should have liked a chat with Kate,' she returned, still struggling for a lightness that would dispel any suspicions he was entertaining about her and Toby.

'Then I'll suggest that she rings you,' he said smoothly. 'I shall be seeing her this evening.'

Her eyes widened in surprise. 'But I thought ... Max, did you forget that I particularly wanted to attend the first night at the Ibex. You promised to get some seats...'

His mouth tightened. 'Oh, I have the tickets,' he said, quite deliberately. 'I'm taking Kate. I expected you to have other plans for this evening as you enjoy your cousin's company so much ... and I am delighted to have the opportunity of entertaining your other cousin. You've set the pattern for the future and I am quite happy to follow it, my dear.'

Her chin tilted at his tone. As if she cared that he wanted to spend his time with her cousin! If only he knew it, he was making things very much easier for her! For if he intended to humiliate her by parading another woman in public so soon after their marriage then she need not feel the slightest qualm about leaving him for another man!

She said brightly: 'I expect we shall get on very much better if we don't live in each other's pockets, Max ... like a great many married couples! We have our own friends and our own interests, after all—just as you pointed out

104

earlier.' She went towards the door. 'I'm a little tired ... I'm going to relax for half an hour before I even think about *my* plans for the evening.'

For all her seeming insouciance, Abigail was badly shaken by his careless acceptance of the situation. She sank on to her bed, discovering that her hands were tightly clenched. She forced herself to relax. It was too ridiculous that she should be so upset ... and over nothing! Why, his indifference played right into her hands! It suited her well that he did not care if she spent every day with Toby ... soon she would go away with him and she need not feel any compassion for the husband she left behind!

But she could not help feeling sick with dismay. She ought to be used to his coldness by now. She ought to have known that once they were no longer dependent on each other for company, Max would follow his own pursuits and pleasures—and expect her to do the same. But it was too bad that he should flaunt Kate of all people under her nose! He must have arranged to meet her that day ... it was unlikely that they had met by chance in an enormous city like London! He must have been as impatient to be with Kate again as she had been to see Toby ... and perhaps for much the same reasons! They had been friends for a long time. Abigail had inevitably wondered if there had been an affair in the past for clever, sophisticated Kate was just his style ... and she might be even more to his taste now that he had sampled marriage with someone like herself, Abigail thought wryly. She had obviously disappointed him ... and perhaps he felt that Kate would gladly give him the ease and comfort that he needed.

Perhaps it was all for the best. She need not worry about hurting him and no doubt he would be relieved when she left. He would hate the public humiliation, of course, and he would probably never forgive her. But he must be as convinced as herself that their marriage was a mistake. She would be happier with Toby— and Max would be free to enjoy himself with Kate or any other woman he wished!

It had been an exhausting day ... and it had ended in a way that she had not foreseen. She was committed to going away with Toby ... and Max was already finding consolation with a woman who was much better suited to him, she told herself—and refused to admit a little core of sadness at the very heart of her. She had reason to be sad. She had made a silly mistake but it was not irrevocable. She should never have married Max ... but he was as much to blame as she was for its failure. He had married her without love and treated her with less than tenderness and made it impossible for her to think of him with any real warmth. If he had been set on turning her against him and putting her off marriage for life, he could not have gone about it more efficiently!

She dawdled in a bath and then relaxed on her bed, sipping the tea that Max's manservant brought at her request. She liked Turner. He was a cheerful Cockney with a fund of good humour and a fatherly manner. She felt that he approved of her and it was comforting. It was easier to talk to Turner and admit her failings where household management was concerned than to consult with Grainger or Mrs Powell about the running of Coneycroft ... they frightened her to death with their superiority! And Turner accepted the fact that she and Max occupied separate rooms without the flicker of an eyelid whereas she sensed that the Coneycroft staff strongly disapproved of the arrangement.

She dozed and was disturbed some time later by the sound of movement in the adjoining room. Max dressing for the evening, she thought drowsily—and then hurt came flooding to startle her with its intensity and unexpectedness.

She ought not to care that he was going out with Kate ... and she would not care if she could believe that it was merely retaliation for the day she had spent with Toby. But Max was unconcerned. Her obvious guilt must have betrayed the fact that her desire to see Toby sprang from more than cousinly affection ... but he was disinterested.

Suddenly she wished that she had found the

107

words to tell Max that she was meeting Toby. It would have been wiser and taken all the horrible, despoiling guilt out of the day. In retrospect, she knew that it had not really been a happy day.

For there was a subtle change in her relationship with Toby that was difficult to define. She could not be comfortable in the knowledge that she had stooped to deceit. Max was entitled to be angry... she only wished he had been angry instead of indifferent. It would have been some indication of affection for her. But she realised that it was nothing to him what she did, where she went, how she spent her time—as long as he could feel equally free!

It was a mockery of marriage, she thought bleakly... and she was to blame. With Toby in her heart and mind, she had turned away from Max at the very time when they ought to have cemented their relationship with a new warmth and intimacy. It was scarcely surprising that there was no hope of any future happiness for them. Angry with herself and resentful of the circumstances that had kept Toby away, she had vented a petulant disappointment on Max ... and probably killed every spark of affection that he might have felt for her! It was not surprising that he had turned to Kate—and she could not condemn him for disloyalty when she carried her own burden of guilt!

Abruptly filled with remorse and a fierce reluctance to admit failure, she wondered if she should retract her promise to Toby and set herself wholeheartedly to the task of saving her marriage. It could not be too late yet ... but a few more days of their estrangement might take them utterly beyond the point of no return.

Impulsively, she called to Max. A moment later, he opened the communicating door, dressed in trousers and a pale blue dress shirt with frilled front and he was inserting cufflinks as he came in answer to her call. 'What is it?' he asked with a hint of impatience.

She felt rebuffed and all her good intentions abruptly deserted her. 'Oh, nothing ... it doesn't matter,' she said stiffly. It was obvious that he had no desire for a reconciliation between them, she thought angrily ... he must feel that she had very little to offer him!

Max frowned slightly. 'Don't play games,' he rebuked coldly. He looked at her, his eyes narrowing. She looked pale, a little frail. 'What is it? Aren't you well?'

She thought bitterly that she would need to be dying before she admitted to needing his comfort and concern ... and marvelled that she had thought it possible to heal the breach between them. He did not want it healed—so why should she strive for a better understanding 'I'm fine,' she said lightly. 'A little tired, that's all. I think I shall stay home, have a leisurely evening...'

'Is that what you wanted to tell me?' Max

turned away for his jacket and thrust his arms into it and then returned to regard her with a polite question in his dark eyes.

He looked very handsome, very masculine—and unexpectedly her heart turned over as she looked at him. It was the strangest feeling—inexplicable and quite indescribable—and it left her oddly shaken. She stared at him, discovering that he was very dear to her, after all—and wondering if she could swallow her pride sufficiently to tell him so. Her emotions were in a turmoil. She was aware of a fierce dislike of their estrangement and a desperate desire to go back to their wedding day and begin all over again with the man she must have alienated with her foolish behaviour. 'No, I . . . Max, can we talk?' she asked impulsively. 'It is important . . .'

He hesitated, reluctant to become involved in a discussion that would probably lead nowhere. He was looking forward to his evening with Kate and did not want anything else on his mind. There were no complications in his relationship with Kate, he thought thankfully. He knew where he was with Kate. She did not play fast and loose with a man's emotions. Heaven knew how he had overlooked all her splendid qualities and made such a fool of himself over her cousin's lovely face!

'Very well,' he said, a little curtly. 'But don't keep me too long, Abigail.'

110

She drew a deep breath and smiled at him, a little tremulously. 'It only takes a minute to say sorry, Max.'

He looked down at her. The apology had come too late and he did not believe she was sincere. She was such a child! She had been caught in deceit and she could not endure disapproval. So she held out the olive-branch of an apology and expected him to forgive and forget all in a moment. Well, it was just not possible. It was not the deception but the motive for it that had struck so savagely at his pride—and it was impossible to think warmly of the girl who had humbled him utterly only to throw his love aside as worthless.

'Words are cheap,' he said harshly. 'Saying sorry doesn't immediately make everything right, you know.'

She flinched at his tone. 'I do know,' she agreed quietly, penitently. 'But I really am sorry ... for everything. I just want a chance to make it up to you, Max.' She held out her hand to him impulsively.

He ignored the outstretched hand. He did not want to touch her. He did not want to kiss the eager, upturned face. He did not want to feel the smallest tug at his heart because of her pale beauty, her spurious sweetness, her warm desirability as she lay against the pillows with the silken mass of her lovely hair framing her small face.

'I don't trust you,' he said curtly. 'You're

111

much too impulsive and you never give any thought to the consequences of your actions. You're just an irresponsible child!'

Hurt swept over her in a tidal wave. The rebuke might be justified but she could not bear the pain it inflicted. Afraid of betraying the effect of his harsh words on a newfound sensitivity, she instinctively took refuge in anger. 'Damn you, Max!' she said sharply. 'I won't eat humble pie again! That's the last time I apologise or explain anything to you!'

He shrugged. 'I'm not the keeper of your conscience.'

Her eyes widened with shock at the indifference of his tone. 'You don't care what I do—is that it?' she demanded resentfully. 'I can go to the devil and you won't lift a finger to stop me, I suppose!'

'You'll do just what you want to do—and I doubt if a team of wild horses could keep you from going to the particular devil who appears to mean more to you than you intended me to know,' he said coldly.

Her chin tilted. 'That's right,' she said with defiance. 'Just as you'll see Kate this evening no matter how I might feel about it, I daresay!'

There was a swift challenge in his dark eyes. 'Do you blame me?' he demanded. 'I have very good reason for wishing to be with a woman who cares about me, wants me! How did I fail you that Cousin Toby seems so attractive?'

She shook her head. It was too involved for

explanation, she thought wryly, knowing in her heart that he only spoke the truth. She had failed him in every possible way and she was entirely to blame for the utter collapse of their marriage.

'You'd better go, Max,' she said quietly, hopelessly. 'Kate will be waiting for you.'

'Yes,' he said, deliberately. 'With open arms...'

They looked at each other like strangers for a moment ... and then he turned and walked out of her room, closing the door with a tiny snap of finality.

There were tears in her eyes and in her heart—and she wondered why she cared so much that it seemed too late to salvage anything from the debris of their relationship. She ought to be thankful for the indifference that made it easy for her to leave him. She ought to be glad that he had already found a degree of satisfaction and contentment with someone else as she already had Toby to love her and look after her. She ought to be relieved that their marriage was so meaningless that it could end without heartache or regret on either side.

She was determined to be thankful, to be relieved—and equally determined that she would not sit meekly at home while he was out with another woman. She did not mean to dwell on what they might be doing, what they might be saying, what they might be feeling for each other while they were together. She would go out herself, enjoy herself, completely forget all about Max and his hurtful indifference!

Within half an hour, she was on her way to join Toby who had been reassuringly eager to alter his arrangements so that they might meet. They went to a cinema and dined and danced at a club in Soho and Abigail did her best to enjoy the evening. After all, she was with the man she loved, she told herself firmly. She had every reason to be happy. She was doing what she wanted to do and enjoying it—and so was Max, presumably! It was a very sensible arrangement and there was not the least need for her to feel guilty! Living one's own life in virtual disregard for the thoughts and feelings of one's partner was apparently the modern recipe for a successful marriage!

But some of the joy had fled from her association with Toby, she found. She studied him with surprising detachment, wondering if living with him would really suit her any better than living with Max. Toby took her so much for granted, she thought wryly. He was affectionate and attentive but she did not feel that she was absolutely necessary to his happiness...

CHAPTER TEN

The conversation revolved about Toby, his achievements, his ambitions ... and Abigail began to realise that although he was willing to allow her some part in his life, he would not be exactly broken-hearted if she decided to stay with Max. He might be very fond of her but he could live quite happily without her, she thought ruefully.

She knew that she had a very real need for emotional security. To be happy, she had to feel that she was needed as well as loved. She could not feel, deep down, that Toby needed her. He was too self-sufficient ... and too selfish. He was a born bachelor, in fact ... the kind of man who did not care to be tied to one person, one place, one way of life. She suspected that he had been swayed by sentiment and gallantry where she was concerned but he could not really want a wife and a settled domestic existence ... he was just not the type!

Whereas Max was basically the kind of man to make an excellent husband if he was given the right encouragement, she thought a little wistfully. They might have been happy if she had not allowed thoughts of Toby and the might–have–been to unsettle her—and Max might not have turned so readily to Kate if she had contented and satisfied him and convinced him that he was necessary to her happiness.

Because Max was very necessary to her happiness, she abruptly knew ... and her heart stood still at the revelation that was like a bolt from the blue. Then it seemed to plummet to the very depths of despair for it was obviously much too late to realise that she wanted nothing more of life than to be loved by the man she had married. He was a man in every sense of the word ... a man to admire, to respect, to love with all her heart—and Toby seemed an immature, irresponsible, utterly selfish boy in comparison!

Remembering her coldness, her rejection, her cruelty to Max, she was horrified and consumed with regret and dismay and a fierce desire to atone. She had behaved despicably—and she had possibly turned away a love that he might have been willing to bestow on her! He had married her out of all the women he knew, many of them much more suitable than herself ... and even Kate had remarked that he must consider her to be 'something special'!

'Take me home, Toby,' she said suddenly, breaking into the account of a party where he had met and impressed a famous film director.

'I must tell you this bit, Abby,' he swept on. 'The great man described a scene in the film, being very complimentary about the fellow who wasn't the star but stole all the thunder...'

'Please, Toby...'

'And he didn't recognise me, Abby! That's the real cream of the joke! So...'

She interrupted again without compunction. 'Tell me another time ... I'm sorry but I must go home. It's very late and I didn't leave any message for Max. He won't know where I am and he may worry.' She spoke lightly ... and only wished she could believe it likely that Max would be concerned!

He raised an amused eyebrow. 'So he should worry! Neglecting you, my sweet! He deserves to get home and find you missing,' he declared. He reached for her hand and raised it to his lips and smiled into her anxious eyes. 'Darling, don't spoil the evening,' he said softly. 'You're wonderful and I love you ... why go back at all? Why make me wait? Where's the point in being miserable with Constantine when you know that I want you. To hell with him!'

Her heart sank slightly. Toby was a dear and she did love him ... but he could not possess the whole of her heart or fill her with an intense longing for his happiness. At last, she knew that real loving was the longing to give and go on giving, totally unselfish in its warmth and generosity, finding all its satisfaction in the well-being and contentment of the beloved. She did not know what had opened her eyes to the truth but she was suddenly absolutely sure that she loved Max and she was desperately impatient to be with him, to beg his forgiveness, to make amends, to do all she could to restore some of the former warmth and intimacy to their relationship.

'I'm sorry,' she said slowly, painfully. 'I've behaved very badly, I know... but I'm not going away with you, Toby. I'm not leaving Max. I can't!'

He searched her rueful face with narrowed eyes. 'Can't ... or won't, Abby?' he asked tersely.

'I couldn't bring myself to humiliate him so badly,' she said carefully. 'There are some things that are quite unforgivable.'

'Do you suppose it won't humiliate him to learn that you're in love with me and only stay with him out of cowardice?' he demanded sharply. 'Don't be a fool, Abby.'

'It isn't cowardice, Toby. It's going to take much more courage to stay with Max than to go away with you, quite frankly.' She drew a deep breath. 'He doesn't love me, you know. I don't think he even likes me any more! I haven't told you very much but our marriage has been disastrous so far—and I have to try to put things right.'

He twisted the gold band on her finger, round and round. 'You're in love with him, Abby,' he said quietly. 'It isn't me at all, is it?'

She was stricken by the pain in his voice. 'Oh, Toby! I've been so stupid, so thoughtless—and I hate myself!' she exclaimed. 'I don't know what to say—what can I say? Sorry is such an inadequate word!'

Impulsively she leaned to kiss his cheek. 'I really thought it was you, Toby—I don't know how or why everything has changed. I don't know why I love Max ... I just know that I do!'

'Convenient,' he drawled ... sounding so much like Max that she was startled. He rose abruptly. 'Very well ... I'll take you home and kiss you goodbye—if that's really what you want!'

Abigail stood in the lift, her heart racing with a strange compound of apprehension and excitement. She had left Toby with an odd little feeling of relief that the foolishness of supposing that she loved and wanted him was at an end...

Turner did not live in, having an invalid sister with whom he shared a flat on the other side of the river. The flat was in darkness. Max might be in bed and asleep, of course ... but Abigail knew with a sick heaviness about her heart that he was not yet home. It was almost two o'clock. She was very late—but Max was even later and she was dismayed. She did not know what his relationship with Kate had been in the past but it would not be surprising if he was in the right mood to cross the threshold from friendship to intimacy, she thought bleakly. Her behaviour had been enough to drive him into another woman's arms, after all!

She wandered about the luxurious flat that was so stamped with his personality. It was very much a man's abode ... a man of taste

119

who liked beautiful things. She could not settle while she waited, longing for him to come home, aching to hear his voice, to know his touch, to have him smile on her with warm liking and friendship if nothing else.

She recalled that they had parted on hostile terms. She recalled the utter coolness, the hurtful indifference ... and she comforted herself with the memory of the Max he had been before she married him, warm and generous and sensitive to her every mood, attentive and considerate and kind. It had seemed so right and natural that she should marry him ... her heart had obviously always known what her foolish head refused to admit, she thought wryly.

She did not think of going to bed. How could she possibly sleep. She was too eager, too impatient, too restless, too anxious ... and too much in love, she thought ruefully, thinking how ironic it was to recognise her need of Max so late in the day. Thank heavens it was not too late! She might have realised the truth after she had gone away with Toby—and that would have been disaster indeed! For she could never have returned to Max and her whole life would have been ruined because of a foolish inability to differentiate between a youthful, sentimental calf-love and a mature and lasting love. Fortunately she had discovered in time where her happiness truly lay—and it was up to her to convince Max!

120

The minutes ticked away. Abigail found herself visualising Max and Kate locked in embrace, forgetful of everything but the ecstasy of the moment—and she clenched her hands so fiercely that the nails cut tiny crescents into her soft palms. She fought the rising tide of jealousy. She must not leap to conclusions. Max was a sensual man, a man of strong passions, but she must not assume that the marriage vows meant little to him just because she had come so near to breaking them! Max was a man of honour and integrity. He was a finer person than she could ever hope to be! He might be fond of Kate and he might respond to the admiration and affection and appreciation that his wife had failed to supply—but Abigail would not believe that he would lightly go to bed with her cousin ... and she leaped thankfully to her feet as her anxious ears caught the sound of the ascending lift. She went eagerly to meet him with flushed face and parted lips ...

Max looked her up and down, noticing the faint smudges of weariness beneath too-bright eyes, the crumpled gown, the tousled hair ... and his lip curled. The shining eyes, the eagerness in her step towards him, the soft colour that tumbled in and out of her small face were easily attributed to guilt and apprehension, he decided.

Throughout the evening, he had been tormented by a vision of Abigail, alone and lonely and wanting him. Wishful thinking, he had told himself drily—but he could not dismiss her from his mind. However hard his heart might be where she was concerned, he did not care for her to be alone in the flat—and it was not like her to have been lying on her bed in the early evening. Deciding that he had been too harsh, too unfeeling, too cold and hostile when she might have been unwell and reluctant to admit it, he had left Kate as soon as he decently could and hurried home.

Concern had abruptly died when he saw the state of her bedroom. Its untidiness told its own story. She had dressed and gone out in haste—probably within minutes of his own departure. She had never intended to go to the theatre with him, obviously. She had carefully laid her plans—and feigned tiredness so that he would not expect her to go out. No doubt she would have urged him to take Kate or someone else in her place if he had not played into her hands, he thought grimly ... and wondered to what strategy she would have resorted if he had decided to stay home!

Too angry for logical thought, he had gone out again ... to look for Abigail in various clubs and casinos and late-night restaurants with little hope of finding her. Now he regarded her coldly, his lips curling ... and he mocked himself for having fallen such an easy victim to her loveliness, her appealing femininity, her warm and enchanting

122

sweetness that had turned out to be such a deceit. If only she had been honest with him. If only she had admitted her love for another man. The wedding could have been cancelled even at the last moment. It would have shattered him but he would have understood, forgiven, admired her honesty—and he would have continued to love her. He could not understand the deception, the treachery, the complete lack of thought and feeling, the mockery of all that marriage stood for ... and he knew that his love for her was like yesterday—gone beyond recall!

'Max...' Abigail found that her courage had deserted her and she could barely speak his name. She had supposed that because she loved him it would not be too difficult to go to him, put her arms about him, tell him that she was truly sorry and ask for another chance, assure him that she wanted his happiness more than anything else in the world. But he did not smile or speak and she was alarmed by the cold implacability of his expression. He looked at her as though she was a stranger that he neither liked nor trusted.

Max was seething. Only the tightest rein on his temper kept him from striking her as she looked at him with that defiant tilt to her chin and that mocking brightness in her eyes, so obviously hot from the hands of her lover! He brushed past her and went to the decanters and poured a stiff whisky. He had drunk too much already but he did not care. A man was entitled to drink himself into a stupor when he knew that he had an unfaithful and unloving wife!

'Why aren't you in bed?' he demanded. 'Don't wait up for me ... ever! There will be nights when I don't come home. There's no shortage of willing women, you know. It's my misfortune that I didn't marry one of them,' he added brutally, throwing himself into a chair. He refused to accept that she flinched at his words. As if she cared what he did—as long as he did not interfere with her pleasures! He closed his eyes, leaning his head against the wing of the chair, desirous of shutting out the pale loveliness of her small face.

Abigail moved towards him ... and paused, wondering why it was impossible to stretch her hand to the crisp head, the lean cheek, the firm shoulder when she loved him so much. She was astonished to realise just how much she loved him and the welling emotion cast her girlish affection for Toby into very pale shadow. She ached to know his arms about her, his lips on her own. But it would be the most difficult thing in the world to make advances to Max, she realised, visualising the irony in his eyes, the sardonic quirk to his mouth, the quizzical lift to his eyebrow when he realised what she was about—and she was afraid of rejection. She must learn to cope with rebuffs, of course—and perhaps in time he would not turn her away if she proved a genuine love and need for him, she thought with the optimism of loving.

With a hammering heart, she moved closer and put out her hand to him ... and drew back swiftly as his eyes opened. Max frowned. He did not want her hovering. She was only waiting to be tackled on the subject of her cousin cum lover, he decided—and he was in no mood for the inevitable showdown. He might lose his temper and then there would be hell to pay!

'Go to bed, girl,' he said impatiently. 'I'm going to get very drunk and I don't want you around!'

She managed a soft little laugh. 'Oh, Max—you'll hate yourself in the morning,' she said lightly. 'Is it worth it?' She smiled at him warmly, finding it even more difficult than she had anticipated. 'Come to bed instead.'

There was veiled insolence in the way his glance slid over her slender body. 'I don't suppose you mean that to be an invitation,' he drawled. 'But, by God, I'd need to be a damn sight drunker than I am to go to bed with an iceberg.'

The colour stormed into her face and her heart swelled with indignation. She loved him—but she had her pride! She went from the room—and stood in the hall with a hand pressed to her mouth to stifle the sob that welled from the depths of her being. A terrible pain seemed to radiate from some deep core

125

and she thought that if she had inflicted even a quarter of this agony on Max, who did not love her, then she could understand why he had turned against her so irrevocably. It took a moment or two before she could cross the hall to her room—and then it was only the dread that Max might find her with tears streaming down her cheeks that gave impetus to her legs. She reached her room and sank on the bed and buried her face in the pillows. It was her first experience of the anguish that could walk hand in hand with loving—and she only had herself to blame!

Max was determined to get drunk ... drunk enough not to care that his wife was a cheat and a wanton, drunk enough to forget the hurt and humiliation she had handed out with no regard for his feelings, drunk enough to blot out the persistent image of her loveliness. The whisky in the decanter sank lower and lower—and he was still disappointingly sober, he told himself wryly, hauling himself to his feet and making his unsteady way to bed. He was very, very tired. He would seek his cold and lonely bed—and everything would be just as bloody in the morning!

Abigail tensed at the sound of a crash. It might only be a chair ... but Max might have fallen. She leaped up, listening—and then went swiftly to the communicating door. Max turned from the mirror where he had been regarding himself in self-mockery, wondering

126

why he had found it easy to win any woman he wanted until he met the cold-hearted Abigail. 'I'm not a bad fellow, Abby,' he said, his voice slurring. 'Women like me. I can get any woman—no trouble at all!' He waved an airy hand and staggered and reached to steady himself—and was surprised to find her shoulder conveniently at hand. He leaned on her heavily and studied her thoughtfully. 'You're a pretty girl,' he said warmly. 'A very pretty girl. You should be in bed—best place for a woman.' He shook his head. 'A man likes to know his woman is waiting at home for him, Abby. You're a good girl, Abby. I thought you'd gone out but you were here all the time, waiting... good girl!'

She guided him to the bed, avoiding the overturned chair. He sat down so suddenly that he almost pulled her with him. He looked about him in surprise, wondering how he had managed to cross the room when his legs suddenly did not belong to him. 'I've a strong head,' he boasted boyishly. 'Couldn't get drunk ... wanted to... wanted to forget—now I've forgotten what I wanted to forget!' He laughed—and then groaned, pressing his hands to his head. 'I don't feel so good,' he admitted wryly.

Abigail ached to hold him close, to stroke the dark head and soothe away the bad feeling, to let her love flow over him. Instead she was practical, helping him out of his clothes, coaxing him to get into bed. As she turned to leave, he caught her wrist. 'Don't go, Abby ... I'm so cold,' he complained. 'Room's going round... don't leave me, Abby.'

'I'm here, Max,' she said quietly. 'Go to sleep...'

'I need you,' he said stubbornly.

She hesitated. Then she slipped beneath the covers and into his arms, her heart beating wildly. He drew her close and nuzzled his face into her neck—but his embrace was entirely sexless. Her heart calmed and she lay against him, relaxed ... and so thankful for the nearness of him which helped to ease the lingering pain and dread in her heart.

In the morning, he might regret and reject her again. Now, he needed her ... and she loved him and she held him with tenderness and delight.

He slept ... and so did she and only stirred when she realised that the heaviness of desire within her was not a dream but the response to the caress of his hands and the warm seeking of his lips and the exciting urgency of his body close to her own...

CHAPTER ELEVEN

Abigail lay and watched the sunlight creep higher and higher as the day advanced. There were pins and needles in her arm where his head rested heavily but she endured rather than disturb him while he slept so peacefully.

She was very conscious of him—and of the delicious afterglow of lovemaking that had swept her to new and unsuspected heights. She had not known that it could be so wonderful and joyous an experience ... but perhaps loving Max accounted for that. She could not believe that sex without love could be so magical, so marvellous.

She was suddenly filled with a warm and tender thankfulness for the man she had married and the certainty that all would be well between them in the future. She turned to him and pressed her lips to his cheek, the corner of his mouth ... and his eyelids flickered. He stirred and murmured something that might or might not have been her name ... and then opened his eyes and looked directly into her own.

'Surprise, surprise,' he said slowly, remembering scarcely anything of the night's events.

She smiled. 'How's your head?' she teased, totally unaware that nothing had really changed ... not for Max, anyway. For Abigail, there had been magic in that dawn encounter. For Max, it had been only relief after too long a deprivation for a man of his sensual nature.

He lay still, regarding her with narrowed eyes ... and although his memory seemed to be clouded his body remembered her nearness and her response to his need. 'Did you put me to bed?' he asked wryly.

'Don't think it was easy!' she said lightly. 'You resisted all the way ... for the first time in your life, I should imagine.' She chuckled.

'I must have been very drunk.'

'Oh, you weren't so drunk,' she assured him softly, her eyes meeting his with warm meaning in their depths.

'We seem to be on speaking terms so I take it that you don't feel that you were forced this time,' he said coolly, rolling away from her to look at the clock beside the bed. 'Lord, it's late!'

'Does it matter?' Her voice held a hint of provocation. She put a tentative hand on his shoulder as he rested on his elbow, turned away from her. 'Max, turn back ... I want to talk to you,' she said softly.

He moved deliberately so that her hand fell away. 'Conversation is not my strong point when it's the morning after the night before,' he said drily. 'Breakfast has more appeal right now.'

She said lightly but with a hint of shyness: 'Perhaps I didn't really have conversation in mind, Max.' She put her arm over him and pressed her lips impulsively to his bare shoulder. 'Max ... ?'

He threw back the covers. 'Breakfast has more appeal, I think,' he reiterated coolly and reached for his robe.

Abigail bit her lip. It had not occurred to her that he would go on hating her, despising her, when they had so recently known such delight in each other's arms. She was so dismayed that she could not think of anything to say ... and he went into the bathroom and turned on the shower.

He felt very much better when he had showered and shaved ... physically, at least. As far as emotion was concerned, he was back to being the unfettered man he had been before he met Abigail, he told himself with relief. She was a very beautiful girl with a very beautiful body but she meant no more than any other woman, after all. The only difference lay in the fact that she wore a wedding ring that he had put on her finger—and if she could forget it so lightly to enjoy herself with Cousin Toby then he could certainly disregard it if another woman chanced to attract him!

He did not know what Abigail wanted... her freedom, perhaps. But Cousin Toby might not be interested in marrying her. Obviously he had not suggested it in the past or Abigail would never have entertained his proposal, Max thought drily. He did not like the idea of a divorce ... it was a public confession of failure. If Abigail agreed to behave with a great deal more discretion in the future and be a conformable wife to him, then he was prepared to close his eyes to her affection for the other man. There was really no reason why they should not live together quite amicably in such circumstances ... like many another couple of his acquaintance...

Abigail toyed with the food on her plate, discovering that she had no appetite. Max ignored her, busy with the morning mail and the newspapers—and one glance at his handsome face told her that he was in an inflexible mood. Nothing had changed, she thought ruefully ... except that she loved him more and had a greater understanding of all that she had lost! She touched his arm on impulse. 'Max,' she said, a little anxiously. 'Max, I think I know how you feel about me— but can I just say that I'm sorry!'

He let the newspaper fall and looked at her without expression. 'Do you suppose that everything can be wiped out with one little word?' he demanded coldly. 'What a child you are!'

The colour came and went in her lovely face. 'It's an inadequate word,' she admitted quietly. 'It doesn't express all that I feel, certainly. I wish you knew how much I mean it.'

He raised an eyebrow. 'Suddenly you have a conscience?' he drawled. 'Or is it another change of heart? You really must make up your mind what it is that you want, Abigail!'

'I know what I want,' she said in a low voice.

'So do I know,' he said drily, rather bitterly. 'Don't take me for a fool! I know what's been on your mind ever since you married me and why you've insisted on separate rooms and why you couldn't wait to get to town. I'm merely curious to know why you seem to be settling for me when I don't believe that I can even aspire to second place in your affections. Doesn't he want you, after all ... Cousin Toby?' The words were a sneer.

Abigail stared down at her hands. She could not meet the mocking challenge in his eyes. For it was all so true. Toby had been constantly on her mind and she had thought it impossible to welcome her husband's embrace and she had been eager to be with the man she foolishly believed that she loved and wanted more than Max ... and if one wanted to be cold and practical and realistic one could certainly say that she had decided to settle for Max and forget all about Toby. But she knew that she had a very real love for him as her motive—and she only wished it was possible to say so and be believed! In his present mood, such an admission would make things worse rather than better, she thought unhappily.

'I suppose you always knew about Toby,' she said quietly, regretfully. There was nothing else she could say. It was pointless to deny that Toby and her imagined love for him was the cause of all the trouble between her and Max.

He had known, of course—but he had not expected her to admit it so brazenly! He was thankful that he had such excellent control over his temper or he might have hit her in that moment. For she showed no shame, no real regret . . . and she was much too confident that he would forgive and forget! He studied her with hard eyes. She must have some reason for wishing their marriage to continue or she would not have slipped into his bed and responded so eagerly to the passion that she had known she could arouse in him . . . and he believed that he had hit the nail on the head with his last words. Joslin had disappointed all her hopes and probably advised her to make the best of her marriage, he decided shrewdly. . . and so the love and the longing must be all on her side. Well, she need not look to him for compassion or concern or comfort!

'Yes, I knew,' he said savagely. 'So does the whole town know, I imagine! I don't give a damn what you do but you must learn to be more discreet or you'll force me to take certain steps that you may not like!'

She glanced at him swiftly, apprehensive. 'Are you talking of divorce?' she asked him in alarm.

'I don't care to advertise my mistakes and I don't think it will suit you to put an end to our marriage,' he said coldly. 'But if you continue to show so little respect for that ring on your finger and so little regard for my position, then I won't hesitate to sue for divorce—and I shall take considerable pleasure in citing Joslin! He won't care for that kind of publicity, I imagine.'

She was very pale. She realised that he could be just as ruthless as the world claimed—and she also knew that he could never have loved her at all. She had never really thought so, of course, but it still hurt that she was so unimportant to him and always had been. 'I wonder why you married me, Max,' she said, a little unsteadily.

He looked at her, considering, remembering, regretting. Then he said quietly: 'I thought you were the loveliest girl I'd ever seen—and I thought you were all that a man could want.' He saw her eyes widen and brighten and swept on with deliberate cruelty: 'But I was mistaken. Your personality doesn't match your lovely face, after all.'

Disappointment came flooding and she flinched as though he had struck her. There was a hint of tears in her eyes and voice but she said evenly:

'You don't give second chances, do you, Max?'

'No, I don't,' he said with steely finality.

She rose abruptly. 'There's no point in going on,' she said, her voice breaking slightly.

He shrugged. 'If that's your decision . . .' He picked up the Financial Times and resumed reading. Abigail pushed back her chair and went swiftly from the room . . . and Max watched her go, his eyes hard and cold. He could not analyse the icy determination within

135

him to punish her in some way. He did not really understand the grim refusal to forgive and forget and try again when she had meant so very much to him such a short time before ... but he knew it was impossible for him to relent, to feel anything for her again...

Abigail threw clothes into a case, scooped things from the dressing-table ... and then stopped in sudden panic. It would be too easy to walk out—and Max would never allow her to return! Was that what she wanted? To leave him, to have their marriage crumble before it had been given any real encouragement to survive, to face the prospect of separation and eventual divorce, to live her life without him?

Max did not want a divorce. He was very proud and no one liked to admit to failure. He was willing to carry on, to allow the world to believe that all was well between them while he actually led his own life and closed his eyes to anything she did as long as she was discreet. The thought of such a life with him appalled but it must be better than losing him altogether!

Matters must improve with time. He could not go on hating and despising her for ever, she told herself with all the optimism of the lover. If she was all that he wanted in a wife—and oh! how she would try to be—perhaps eventually he would again feel some degree of affection for her, she thought wistfully. She did not expect him to love her ... that was beyond her wildest dreams! But surely they could learn to live together in affection and amity?

She soon discovered that it was far from easy to live with him at all and strive to win back his liking and respect. She had thought him cold and impersonal at Coneycroft. But he had been warm and tender and even loving in contrast to his attitude towards her, now. She tried very hard to accept, to make allowances, to be patient and understanding ... but he did not give an inch! He spent as little time as possible in her company. He was long hours at the office and long hours in his study when he was home ... Abigail was free to do as she pleased and go where she wished—but she did not want to do anything without Max and there was no pleasure in the social round if he did not share it with her. It became increasingly difficult to explain to friends and family why Max was almost always absent from her side ... even the busiest of men could usually find a little time for family and social commitments. She began to refuse invitations, to avoid her friends, to spend too many hours on her own. She was unhappy, depressed because Max did not seem to notice or care, and she never felt really well. It was a little puzzling for she had always been bursting with health and vitality. She had no appetite. She did not sleep well. She was losing weight and there were faint shadows beneath her eyes and a constant sickness at her stomach that she attributed to the frustration of loving and longing for a man who showed not the smallest sign of affection for her.

Max noticed the changes and hardened his heart, attributing her obvious unhappiness and tension to the fact that she had been disappointed in love. He did not doubt that she still yearned after Cousin Toby. It seemed that the man had neatly extricated himself from their affair and gone to America at the earliest moment. Max refused to feel sorry for Abigail. Her mistake lay in marrying the wrong man and she must pay the penalty, he thought harshly. It would do her no harm to suffer a few pangs and she was young enough to recover without scars. When she was ready to forget her youthful infatuation for her cousin, he might relent and allow himself to become fond of her again. But he would not commit himself to fresh heartache until he was sure that she no longer loved the man who had come close to destroying their marriage. It survived—but only just.

They continued to live together but Max led his own life almost as though he was still a bachelor and took very little interest in Abigail's activities. When it was unavoidable he escorted her to social functions and played host at their dinner table and outwardly appeared the attentive husband and she made the effort to play her part in the charade. She made no demands on him at all … and he seemed to have no time for his unsatisfactory wife. Yet she suspected that he had a great deal of time for Kate and she came near to hating the cousin that she had always liked and admired so much. The gulf between them grew wider with every passing day ... and Abigail felt more and more wretched. She was deeply in love. She had never supposed it possible to be so committed to loving and she could only marvel that she had so foolishly confused her affection for Toby with the all-consuming emotion that was her love for the man she had married.

Max realised that matters must eventually come to a head between them. He knew that they could not continue indefinitely with a marriage that was no marriage at all. He waited to know what Abigail meant to do ... and suspected that only lack of courage and acute dislike of public speculation kept her from leaving him. She could not really wish to stay with him in the circumstances, he felt. It was obvious that she did not have a scrap of real affection for him or she would make some effort to heal the breach between them. Of course, the original motive for marrying him must still survive but he did not think that she enjoyed being Lady Constantine as much as she had expected. The wealth, the social standing, the privileges of rank might be very pleasant but they seemed to be outweighed by the necessity of spending her life with the man who provided such things!

Sometimes Max tried to recall the emotion he had known and which he had believed to be real and lasting love for Abigail. But he could only recapture the intensity of sexual longing and that survived to torment him. There were times when he hungered for his wife ... and those were the times when he spoke to her with even colder courtesy and made a point of avoiding her company. In the past it had never occurred to him that loving was an essential part of lovemaking but his attitudes had changed abruptly and he had no heart for cold-blooded sex ... and Abigail did not give him encouragement or opportunity to overcome his scruples, he thought wryly.

He had a fierce dislike of divorce. He knew there were circumstances which made it inevitable at times ... and he did not condemn those who felt they could not continue with an unhappy state of affairs. But he had always felt that if he ever married it would be for ever, come what may ... and he still felt that he and Abigail could reach a new understanding in time if they both wished for it. Perhaps she wanted a divorce in which case he would not stand in the way of a happiness she might be able to find with someone else ... but he had no wish to end their marriage and the suggestion of divorce would not come from him, he determined. Abigail was far from being the kind of wife he had dreamed and believed she would be—but she was still his wife! The lovely, sweet-natured, enchanting girl he had adored had been only a figment of his imagination ... but perhaps a new kind of love would dawn one day for the woman she really was ...

CHAPTER TWELVE

Abigail woke one morning, feeling slightly sick and headachy, utterly dispirited ... and suddenly she knew a yearning for Coneycroft that surprised her. Then she recalled its quiet and pleasant and very peaceful atmosphere, its beautiful surroundings, its many enjoyable pursuits ... and compared it with the hot stickiness of town in midsummer and the demands of the social round that seemed to weary her so much of late.

It would be nice to go down to Coneycroft and spend a few weeks really getting to know her new home, she decided ... and recalled wistfully that she and Max had not been at such loggerheads when they stayed there soon after their wedding. He had been kind and considerate and thoughtful then ... and she marvelled that she had been so impatient and restless and resentful. If only she had realised her love for him and how important it was that he should have no cause to regret marrying her, she thought unhappily. Perhaps they could recapture some of the warmth and friendliness of those days, she thought with sudden optimism. Nothing had gone right between them since they came to town and she had developed a fierce distaste for the penthouse apartment for all its comfort and luxury and convenience. It was not a home, she felt ... and it certainly did not provide the right kind of atmosphere to warm Max's cold heart where she was concerned!

She approached him after breakfast. He was in his study, dark head bent over a sheaf of important-looking papers, and he glanced up with some impatience as she entered. She wondered wryly if he would ever smile and hold out his hand and welcome her with warmth in his attractive voice as he had been used to do. He might never have loved her but he had certainly been very fond of her in those days ... and she had killed all his affection, all his trust, with one act of folly. He was hard, unforgiving ... and he did not give second chances. But she knew that he would not have attached the slightest importance to her meeting with Toby that day or her confessed affection for him if she had been the warm and loving wife that he had been entitled to expect.

She tried to smile but the smile slid away before the indifference in his eyes. 'Can you spare a moment, Max?'

'Of course,' he said with cold civility ... but he did not set aside the documents he was studying and it was apparent from his manner that it would only be a moment of his time that she could expect.

'I think I should like to go home, Max,' she said ... and there was a wealth of yearning in her voice for the place she had never supposed she could ever think of as her home. It was strange that she was seized with this desperate need for a place that she scarcely knew ... but perhaps not so strange when one remembered that Max had been born at Coneycroft, grown up through infancy, boyhood, adolescence and into maturity in the big house and it seemed that she might get closer to the man she had married in the surroundings that had helped to shape his character and personality. She was suddenly confident that everything could come right if only they went back to Coneycroft.

He frowned, scarcely knowing whether to be thankful or regretful that she had finally reached a decision. Actually, he felt nothing but a sense of loss—but that had been inevitable from the beginning.

He said steadily: 'Are you sure it's what you want, Abigail?'

'Oh yes!'

He nodded. 'Very well. I daresay it's the best thing all round.'

She toyed with a heavy glass paperweight on his desk. 'I do feel that I want to get away, Max,' she said earnestly. 'We aren't very close these days and something must be done to

143

mend matters. I know I can't go on like this.'

'I agree,' he said carelessly. 'I think we need a break from each other, certainly … and a short separation might help matters.'

He was so impersonal that her heart faltered and she was deeply disappointed that he obviously had no intention of accompanying her to Coneycroft. She knew that he was a busy man with many demands on his time and attention but there was no reason why he could not handle his business affairs from the country estate and only use the town flat on occasions.

'I suppose you have lots of meetings—and other commitments,' she said tentatively.

He smiled … a cool, rather mocking little smile. 'I won't miss you, Abigail,' he said drily.

Her heart contracted. She knew it was true but he might have pretended otherwise, she thought a little bitterly. It was very hard work trying to make a marriage work all on one's own … Max simply did not help at all! She supposed he really did not have any interest in its state of health … and it seemed that he did not allow it to interfere very much with his way of life!

She said on a sudden impulse: 'No, I know—but I might miss you, Max.'

She sounded so youthful, so wistful that he was torn between impatience and a surprising wave of tenderness. He wondered if she would ever know what she really wanted out of life.

She was still a child at heart and although there was some degree of appeal in that character trait it could also be very irritating, he thought wryly. 'Then you may come back,' he said lightly, his tone betraying how unlikely he thought it to be.

'Yes,' she said, trying hard to keep the disappointment from her tone. 'I'll go this morning, I think.'

'Just as you wish,' he returned carelessly as though it was an everyday event for a wife to walk out on her marriage. He glanced at his watch and then at the telephone on his desk. 'I'm sorry but I really am very busy, Abigail,' he said dismissively. 'I'm expecting a call from Louis and I have to check these figures before I talk to him.'

'When ... when will I see you?' she asked brightly as though it was of little importance whether it was days or months before they were together again.

He realised that she would wish to discuss the legal formalities of separation but he did not see the need for any haste in the matter. 'I shall be involved with the Paris commitment for some days,' he said smoothly. 'Then I'm off to Amsterdam for a week or so ... I'm not really sure when we can meet. Your decision comes at a very convenient time, actually. I shall have even less time to devote to a wife and I know you'll be in good hands. I'll be in touch with you, Abigail,' he added as the telephone shrilled and he reached for it with a dismissive nod for her.

She did not want to go down to Coneycroft without him but he so obviously felt relieved to be rid of her that she knew that she had no choice now. She could only hope that he would miss her, after all—and join her at Coneycroft in the very near future.

On impulse, she stooped to press her lips to his lean cheek, her heart thudding with the fear that he might instinctively rebuff her kiss. 'Bye, Max,' she said with admirable lightness considering how wretched she felt . . . and fled.

Max touched a hand to his cheek in some surprise. That fleeting kiss was their only physical contact in a long time and its obvious impulsiveness, hinting at regret, caught unexpectedly at his heart. But Louis was very voluble and very French in his ear, demanding his entire attention—and he dismissed the fleeting fancy that he would miss his beautiful wife much more than pride would allow him to admit . . .

It was a little awkward for Abigail to arrive at Coneycroft without Max, knowing that the staff had a strong suspicion that all was not well between them, but she airily explained that he had business in Paris and Amsterdam and would be out of the country for several days and she had felt that Coneycroft must be more attractive than town in the middle of a long hot summer.

She told herself that Coneycroft was her home and she must learn to deal with Grainger and Mrs Powell in her new role as its mistress. Max would be pleased if she proved herself to be capable and efficient in the management of the big house, she felt—and she wanted very much to please him, to prove that she could be the kind of wife he wanted.

The days passed ... lonely days that Abigail tried to fill without resentment at Max's continued absence and silence. It seemed that he did not wish to see her, to be with her, even to talk to her ... and she wondered if he looked upon their present separation as a prelude to divorce and was busily reshaping his life without her. She telephoned several times without success, leaving messages with Turner and his secretary that Max obviously chose to ignore. She gritted her teeth and endured and forced herself to patience and struggled with the fierce pangs of loving and longing and loneliness ... and marvelled that anyone could care as little as Max cared for her. But she refused to despair...

While Max threw himself into a flurry of work, discussing and planning and organising a new venture with his business associates ... and had no idea that his wife was hopelessly awaiting his arrival at Coneycroft. It simply did not occur to him that she might have been referring to Coneycroft when she talked of 'home' and he supposed that she had simply

147

decided that there was no future for their farce of a marriage and left him, expecting him to get in touch with her through her family when he felt so inclined.

He had yet to feel so inclined. He felt that there was no point in post-mortems. Their marriage had been virtually stillborn—and it was just one of those things. He decided that it would cause very little surprise or speculation when it became known that they had parted. His friends had known better than himself that he was more suited to the bachelor life than to marriage ... and her friends would declare spurious sympathy for the girl who had failed to convince him otherwise!

He was busy with a great many business matters and he relaxed only in the masculine atmosphere of his club, spending little time at the flat which seemed to echo with a strange emptiness now that Abigail had gone although he had not supposed that she could have impressed it with her personality in a few short weeks. He carefully avoided friends and acquaintances who might ask questions, issue invitations and would certainly assume that he and Abigail were together and enjoying married life. He did not even see Kate for he might be tempted to pour all his troubles into her sympathetic ear and ease his disappointment and frustration in her sympathetic arms. He told himself there was absolutely nothing to keep him from going to bed with Kate or any other woman—but he could not muster any enthusiasm for the idea and decided that his experience with Abigail had effectively put him off sex for the time being.

He was not often at the flat except to collect his mail, change his clothes or snatch the occasional meal ... and he was surprised to be constantly greeted by Turner with the information that Abigail had telephoned. He accepted all messages carelessly, leaving Turner with the impression that he would immediately ring his wife ... and proceeded to do nothing of the sort. Turner obviously assumed that he knew where Abigail was and she never left a number where she could be reached! He had neither time nor inclination to ring round all her family and friends in the attempt to locate her ... and he did not feel that they had anything of importance to say to each other. Eventually she would telephone or call at the flat when he was there ... or he would casually discover her whereabouts from some source and contact her. There was no urgency in the matter. It would be some time before divorce proceedings could be set in motion. In the meantime, he had a great deal to occupy his attention and he could not be concerned with his runaway bride...

Abigail walked slowly along the pavements in the hot sunshine, trying to marshal her thoughts and emotions, a slender figure in the brown trouser suit that emphasised the pale beauty of hair and skin. Heads turned as she passed but she was unaware of evoking admiration and interest. She was on her way to see Max at his office...

She had travelled up to town that morning for two reasons. No word from Max for so long seemed to imply that their marriage was past saving as far as he was concerned ... and the suspicion that she was pregnant had brought her swiftly for a consultation with the Harley Street doctor who had brought her into the world. Too early to be certain, he had said with old-fashioned amusement at her insistence on a positive answer ... and reminded her that she was recently married and it was not unusual for these little alarms to prove meaningless in such circumstances. He had been reassuring—but it was not reassurance that she sought. She wanted to be sure! Deep down, she was sure—and desperately anxious for the breach between her and Max to be healed before it became obvious that she was pregnant! If he once got into his head that she only wanted to save her marriage because she carried his child, she would never be able to convince him that she loved and needed him beyond anything else in the world!

He would be pleased about the child, she told herself hopefully. He would hope for a boy, of course—the heir he must want for all his denials, the heir for which he had presumably married her. It was too new and a little too frightening for Abigail to know if she was pleased ... and it was not at all as she had planned in her youthful dreams of marriage and motherhood, she thought wryly. It was much too soon, for one thing. She had hoped to be rather more used to being a wife before she became a mother! But it would be months before the child was born and surely she and Max could recapture something of the relationship they had known before they married and redeem some of the misery and misunderstanding of recent weeks.

She wanted so much to see him. She had missed him terribly during the three weeks she had spent at Coneycroft without him ... and she would not have believed it possible that he could ignore her very existence for so long and so entirely—or that she could be so patient and tolerant and undemanding! She had been surprisingly content at Coneycroft despite the nagging ache of missing Max and the deep-rooted fear that he was happier without her. Perhaps she had needed those few weeks to herself. Certainly she felt that she had acquired a new maturity and a new understanding of many things. Most of all, she had gained a new insight into the man she had married from living in the house where he had been born and raised, from talking to people on the estate who had known and loved him from boyhood, from listening to all the family history related by Mrs Powell who had unbent considerably when she realised that Abigail was really interested in Coneycroft and the Constantines and was really in love with her husband.

Her heart quickened as she neared the modern block where Max had his office. Learning from Turner that Max had a conference that morning and would be dining out that evening, she had realised that if she wanted to see him that day she must catch him at the office. He had been so elusive in the last few weeks that she could not doubt that he was deliberately avoiding contact with her and it was not going to be easy to thrust herself on his notice, she thought wryly. As yet, she did not know what she would say to him—but she meant to swallow the last of her pride and make it as obvious as possible that she loved him and could not be happy without him. Her heart was too full of love to allow any room for the foolish pride that could easily wreck a marriage...

Yet she almost fled from the office when it transpired that Max was in conference and would not be disturbed. His secretary looked apologetic as she replaced the telephone. Abigail smiled at her as though the obviously curt message from her busy husband had not smote her to the heart.

'I'll wait,' she said lightly, carelessly, and sat down on a leather couch and picked up a magazine, looking very much more confident and serene than she felt.

Miss Marshall was thoughtful, ordering coffee and biscuits—and Abigail sensed a hint of sympathy in the woman's attitude and wondered if she felt that a recently-married man ought to have ignored the demands of business and rushed to welcome his wife with open arms. Yet as his secretary for several years, she should know that Max was not a man to show his feelings in public ... and Abigail mentally added that he was not a man to show his feelings in private, either! She had never really known how much, if anything, he cared about her. But she had never doubted that he wanted very much to marry her, she abruptly recalled. He had looked forward to their wedding with a very real intensity ... and it puzzled her now, remembering. But she resisted the temptation to fancy that he might have loved her then—and told herself firmly that she would be the happiest woman in the world if he came to love her only a little in the years ahead!

CHAPTER THIRTEEN

Max was a businessman and he did not allow the tugging of personal affairs to hasten the end of the conference. There was much to be discussed and much to be settled and a certain

153

amount of opposition to overcome ... and he finally shook hands with his associates and left them feeling as satisfied as he felt with the conclusions they had reached.

Then he allowed himself to think of Abigail and to wonder what had brought her to the office when they might have met and talked things over in a variety of other places. Perhaps she was aiming for the impersonal touch, he thought wryly.

He strode into the room and tossed his briefcase on to a filing cabinet, spoke briefly to Miss Marshall and then turned to Abigail who had laid down her magazine to look at him expectantly as he entered. He stood very still, studying her ... for the very briefest of moments that seemed an eternity to the girl whose heart pounded in her throat. Then he smiled and went to her and bent to kiss her cheek—and her heart lifted with relief and delight. It was the first gesture of spontaneous affection that she had known from him in much too long and foolishly she supposed that he was pleased to see her. Then she realised the cool detachment in his dark eyes, so untouched by his smile, and knew that the incident was entirely for his secretary's benefit!

Max touched his lips to the smooth cheek and resisted the fancy that he had missed her. In fact, he had managed very well without her, he told himself firmly. They had been together for too short a time for his life to have changed radically and it had reverted to its former ease and comfort with her departure. So he declared to himself, anyway, too proud to admit that she might still matter to him, after all...

'My dear,' he said lightly, carelessly, as though it was only a few hours since he had seen her. 'You shouldn't have waited ... you know how these conferences can drag on!'

'I wanted to see you, Max,' she said with equal lightness as though it was not the urgency of that wanting that had brought her all the way from Berkshire despite the fear of rejection. She put aside the magazine and rose to her feet and tucked her hand into his arm, looking up at him with appeal in her eyes, secure in the knowledge that he would not rebuff her while Miss Marshall looked on. 'Spare me a few moments from your busy day.'

'Of course,' he returned, a little stiffly, reminding himself that she was still his wife and entitled to some of his time if that was all she wanted. 'Miss Marshall, intercept all calls for the time being, please.' He threw open the door of his inner sanctum and ushered Abigail out of sight and hearing of the sentimental Miss Marshall.

Abigail felt slightly sick, a little shaky. Now that she had cornered him she did not know what to say to him. All the carefully rehearsed speeches had fled from her mind.

Max went to stand by the window. He had supposed that he could face her with

155

equanimity when they met but he discovered that she still had the power to stir something in him ... the recollection and the resentment of hurt, he believed. He had loved her so dearly ... so much that he could not forgive her utter disregard for the strength and the depth of his feeling for her. He had never loved any woman before her and he did not think that such an emotion could be experienced twice in a lifetime. There was only one Abigail for him— and they might have been very happy if he had been able to blind himself to the faults and follies of the lovely girl he had married.

Abigail looked at the broad, uncompromising back—and her heart sank. He did not mean to make it easy for her, she realised. 'You're very elusive,' she said, striving for lightness. 'I suppose you were getting my messages?'

'I've been in and out of the country ... very busy, in fact,' he said, a little curtly, not even glancing in her direction.

'But you knew I was trying to get in touch with you?' she persisted gently.

'Yes, I knew.'

'You didn't ring me,' she said, trying to keep all hint of reproach from her tone.

'I've been very busy,' he said again.

'Too busy even to talk to me,' she said quietly. 'I'm sorry you feel like that, Max.' She forced herself to move to his side, to stand by him, to smile into the cold, discouraging eyes that now met her own albeit reluctantly. 'I've missed you,' she said almost abruptly.

He raised a cynical eyebrow. 'I wish I could believe you!'

'You don't want to believe me!' she returned with a spurt of spirit.

'Perhaps I just don't trust you any more,' he said coldly. 'Now ... what is it you want? Why are you here? You haven't waited half an hour just to tell me an obvious lie.'

Her heart swelled. But she reminded herself that she had known it would not be easy. 'I wanted to see you,' she reminded him, smiling. 'I have to talk to you, Max.'

He shrugged. 'Talking won't mend matters.'

'Nor will pretending that I don't exist,' she pointed out as calmly as she could. 'You can't sweep me under the carpet, you know. I'm your wife.'

'When you care to remember it,' he said coldly.

She looked at him, her eyes dark with pain and longing. Impulsively she touched her hand to his lean cheek and there was tenderness in the gesture. 'You're so hard, Max,' she said quietly, ruefully. 'Did I do that to you—or were you always so cold and unfeeling and I just didn't know it!'

He moved impatiently from her touch, resenting the fact that she could still quicken his senses and perhaps even his heart, instinctively suspicious of the melting softness

157

that she had never shown towards him in all the weeks of their marriage. It tempted him to forget the hurt and humiliation and remember only the warmth and sweetness and seeming goodness that had inspired him to a very real loving. 'Abigail, you obviously came to say something that you feel is important. Please say it and go!'

She bit her lip. 'I can't find the words,' she said, so quietly that he almost did not hear. He stared down at her, frowning, suspicious, hostile, far from melting before the warm tide of love that rose in her and which she could not express in speech. Suddenly, with a little catch in her breath, she put her arms about him and reached up to kiss him. Taken by surprise, he suffered the touch of her lips for a moment ... and then he drew away. 'Hold me, Max,' she pleaded. 'Please hold me ... I need you so much.' She clung to him, almost desperately, while his arms remained by his sides and there was not a trace of response in his expression or in the stiffness of his body. 'I love you so,' she said hopelessly, achingly.

He was silent.

'I love you,' she said again, a little desperate with the need to convince him. 'Please listen ... please believe me! I love you, Max! I need you! I can't bear being away from you—truly I can't!' Her heart broke with the emotion that wrenched the words from her heart ... and still he looked down at her without expression, without even a flicker of response. Her arms fell away from him abruptly. 'You don't believe me,' she said bleakly.

She was very tense, very taut, aching with tears that could never erase or ease the terrible pain in her breast.

Max walked to his desk and picked up a pen, needing something to occupy his hands that might betray him by reaching for her despite the urging of his head that it would be folly to obey the impulse of his heart all over again. 'I'm inclined to believe that you believe it,' he said carefully. 'I just wonder why you need to persuade yourself that you love me, after all. Obviously you want to come back to me—and you've a reason. I'm sure you don't do anything without a very good reason, in fact.'

'How can you be so cold-blooded?' she asked wearily, knowing that it had been a mistake to come, to try to mend matters. If he had ever felt the smallest glow of affection for her it was utterly dead, utterly beyond recall. She looked at him, wishing with all her heart that it was possible to turn back the clock. Oh, to be happily anticipating her wedding to a man that she had not realised that she loved so much although every instinct had urged her to marry him. 'You don't care at all, do you?' There was anguish in her tone and tears brimming on her lashes.

Max could not look at her. She was so young, so vulnerable, so appealing and she wrenched at his heart. But he must not be swayed by foolish sentiment. Once he had loved her deeply but all that emotion had been destroyed when he discovered that she was not the girl he believed her to be ... and he did not want to love her again.

'What do you expect?' he demanded roughly. 'You turned our marriage into a mockery—and then you left because I wouldn't play the game by your rules! Now you appear to have decided that you love me ... I suspect that it's a matter of expedience rather than emotion. I wonder what you really missed, Abigail ... I don't believe it was me!'

She sighed. 'You're determined to hate me, Max. I can't talk to you! I can't get through to you! It really is finished, isn't it? If you still cared about me or our marriage you'd have come down to Coneycroft to be with me instead of behaving as if I didn't even exist...'

'Coneycroft?' he echoed sharply, startled. 'When were you at Coneycroft?'

'All the time, of course,' she said, staring at him in surprise.

'I don't understand ... when did you go to Coneycroft—and why?'

'The why must be obvious,' she returned drily. 'It is my home now, Max ... that's how I feel, anyway. And I went there when I said I was going ... the day I left town. I expected you to follow me in a few days.' She looked at him with eyes that were suddenly as hard as his

160

own. 'Where do you think I've been, Max ... or didn't it even occur to you to wonder?'

He looked at her steadily and with a hint of rue in his dark eyes. He supposed she must have made it clear that she was going to Coneycroft if only he had taken time off from business matters to listen! He had been so intent on keeping her out of the forefront of his mind and heart, so intent on punishing her for all the hurt she had inflicted on him, so intent on maintaining the cold formality that was meant to protect him from further hurt—and he had deliberately ignored her obvious regret, her gentle efforts at reparation, her transparent need for a reconciliation. It seemed that he had hurt her with his coldness, his deliberate neglect, his attitude of dislike and indifference ... and while he had wished to punish her he had never really supposed that he caused her any real heartache.

It was a shock to hear words of love on her lips ... and he was not sure that he believed or welcomed her declaration of love. She might have made him the happiest of men with the gift of her love only a few weeks before, he thought wryly ... now it was much too late. Yesterday love could be remembered but never recalled.

His silence brought an angry flush to her cheeks. 'I see,' she said stiffly. 'You thought I was with Toby, obviously.'

'No,' he said truthfully. 'I didn't think that,

161

Abigail. I knew your cousin had gone back to Hollywood some time ago. But I certainly thought that he had a great deal to do with your decision to go away.'

'He certainly had a great deal to do with the collapse of our marriage,' she said wearily. 'Oh, Toby wasn't really to blame, of course. I expect you were right when you said I was just a child and that I wasn't ready for marriage with any man. I seem to have grown up a lot in a short time ... but apparently I've grown up too late. Thinking I loved Toby caused all this trouble between us and I don't know how to put things right. I can't do it on my own—and you are determined not to help,' she added, her eyes very bleak as despair suddenly swept over her. For there was no encouragement in his attitude, absolutely no hope for the future. She sighed. 'I ought to have left you, Max,' she said abruptly. 'I ought to have gone right away and tried to forget you. I'm an awful idiot, aren't I? Loving you, wanting you, waiting patiently for you to come home and make all right with one word, one kiss...' She laughed and it was a harsh, painful little sound. 'It might happen like that in romantic novels—but you aren't at all romantic, are you, Max? You don't know anything about love, do you? You don't believe in it, I daresay.' Her voice rose slightly on a note of hysteria. 'You only married for the sake of an heir, didn't you? Everyone said so and of course it was true although I didn't want

162

to believe it and you denied it. Well, you should be delighted to hear that I'm pregnant!'

Max stiffened and then moved swiftly to seize her chin and tilt her face with rough fingers so that he could look into the defiant eyes that sparkled with unshed tears. 'Mine?' he demanded involuntarily, tense with the need to know, to be sure ... and could have bitten out his foolish tongue even as he spoke. For he knew in his heart and mind and deep in his being that she had never belonged to any man but himself. Wave upon wave of bitter regret swept over him for all the wasted weeks, all the foolishness of love without trust, all the mishandling of the warm, impulsive, generous heart that Abigail possessed and which she might have given into his keeping so much sooner, so much more gladly if he had made more allowances for her youth and simplicity and confused emotions.

Abigail raised a hand and dashed it across his handsome face with all her strength, stricken to the very heart of her being by his dismaying doubt of her integrity. The marks of her fingers stood out as angry weals on his lean cheek and she did not wait for reaction or retaliation. She fled, dashing past the startled Miss Marshall, thinking of nothing but the desperate need to escape from the shock and the horror and the agony. She buzzed for the absent lift and then, too impatient to wait and determined not to be called back by a furious

Max, she turned to the stone stairway and flew down it at reckless speed.

So reckless that one of her heels caught on the edge of a stair and she could not keep herself from falling although she reached frantically for the rail . . . and Max found her in a tumbled heap and his heart stood still with fear. He gathered her slight unconscious body into his arms with tenderness and knew beyond a shadow of doubt that a love such as he felt for Abigail could not be banished to the past but would be a vital part of him into eternity and beyond . . .

Abigail drifted between two worlds for several days . . . and she woke to pain and a feeling of emptiness and a terrible weariness. Max was by her side, tense and subdued and anxious, clasping her hand in both of his own as though he feared she might slip away from him for ever.

Relief lightened the shadows in his handsome face as her eyes flickered and opened and looked directly into his own with real understanding at last. 'Thank God . . . !' he said quietly and lowered his dark head to rest on her arm for a moment, abruptly overcome by emotion.

Abigail knew that she had needed him and he had not failed her . . . he had been constantly by her side, supporting and comforting her. She knew that she had called him and known immediately the reassuring touch of his hand

and the quiet murmur of his voice. She knew, without being told, that she had lost the child she had been carrying and that Max felt the disappointment as deeply as she did. Most important of all, she knew that he loved her and that he had suffered with her during those dark hours and her heart welled with deep and lasting love for him.

She stroked the dark hair and said softly, tenderly: 'I'm so sorry, Max.'

He lifted his head and was no less a man to the woman who loved him because tears stood in his dark eyes. 'So am I, Abby,' he said quietly and the words were heartfelt. He raised her hand to his lips and a wealth of love betrayed itself in the way that he smiled at his lovely wife. 'My darling, I've been very stupid, very stubborn and much too proud—and all because I love you so much. My lovely, lovely Abigail ... you mean all the world to me and I've been so afraid...' He broke off, choking on words that he could not even bear to think let alone utter.

'Max I'm fine now,' she said bravely. 'You mustn't worry any more! Poor Max, you look as if you haven't slept in days.'

He smiled wryly. 'I don't think I have,' he admitted.

She put an arm about his neck and drew him down so that she could kiss him ... and her lips were very warm, very sweet on his own. 'I want to come home, Max,' she said wistfully. 'I want to be with you...'

He drew her close to his heart. 'You are never without me, my darling,' he said gently. 'My love surrounds you night and day as it has from the moment I met you and knew you for my own. Come what may, my love is yours, Abby ... yesterday, now and forever...'

We hope you have enjoyed this Large Print book. Other Chivers Press or G. K. Hall Large Print books are available at your library or directly from the publishers. For more information about current and forthcoming titles, please call or write, without obligation, to:

Chivers Press Limited
Windsor Bridge Road
Bath BA2 3AX
England
Tel. (01225) 335336

OR

G. K. Hall
P.O. Box 159
Thorndike, Maine 04986
USA
Tel. (800) 223–6121 (U.S. & Canada)
In Maine call collect: (207) 948–2962

All our Large Print titles are designed for easy reading, and all our books are made to last.